Praise for *The Freeze-Frame Revolution*

"Peter Watts is a brilliant bastard of a science fiction writer, whose grim scenarios are matched by their scientific speculation; in his latest, a novella called *The Freeze-Frame Revolution*, Watts imagines a mutiny that stretches out across aeons, fought against a seemingly omnipotent AI. This is definitely vintage Watts, from the Elder Gods the Eri discovers as it traverses the wormholes it creates, to the imaginative tortures the mutineers use to punish those who betray the rebellion."
—Cory Doctorow, author of *Little Brother* and *Walkaway*

"A gripping story of a deep human future—the dependent relationship between human and AI tangles and grows with the delicious creep of suspense to the very last page. Watts is a poet when it comes to science."
—Justina Robson, author of *Keeping it Real*

"If you ever doubted that the core of all good science fiction is still the human heart, here comes Peter Watts to ram the point home. *The Freeze Frame Revolution* is the purest driven high concept SF, told across scales of time and space to daunt all but the very finest Space Opera practitioners, and yet it remains as vivid and carnal and profane as the headiest of high-end literature."
—Richard Morgan, author of *Altered Carbon*

"Darkness and awesome technology lurk in *The Freeze-Frame Revolution*."
—Vernor Vinge, author of *A Fire Upon the Deep*

"Watts takes familiar-seeming SF tropes and accelerates them towards lightspeed, until they become something chillingly other. A gripping tale where galactic timescales collide with biology and age-old human dilemmas."
—Hannu Rajaniemi, author of *Summerland* and *The Quantum Thief*

"Fast, rich, and cool—*The Freeze-Frame Revolution* fascinates!"
—Greg Bear, author of *Eon* and *Take Back the Sky*

"In *The Freeze-Frame Revolution*, Peter Watts takes us millions of years into the future and hundreds of light-years away, where an isolated fragment of humanity must confront exotic physics, unfathomable entities, and the unforeseen consequences of their own technologies . . . A brilliant, thoughtful story bursting with radical ideas."
—David D. Levine, author of the Arabella of Mars trilogy

"*The Freeze-Frame Revolution* is a slow-motion rebellion as heart-stopping as any roller coaster ride and will delight readers across the science fiction spectrum. It was a joy to read and I found myself unable to put it down once I got started."
—K. B. Wagers, author of *Before the Throne*

"Entertaining and provocative, brilliant and ambitious, *The Freeze-Frame Revolution* is compelling science fiction with heart."
—*Foreword*, starred review

"Peter Watts is a triple threat: exacting hard science extrapolation, an imagination that runs hot enough to give you contact burns, and a gift for thrusting his characters in situations that will expand the mind while shattering even the most guarded of reader hearts."
—A. M. Dellamonica, author of *Indigo Springs*

Praise for Peter Watts

"A new book from crazy genius Watts is always cause for celebration . . . Watts is one of those writers who gets into your brain and remains lodged there like an angry, sentient tumor."
—*io9*

"[Watts] asks the questions that the best science fiction writers ask, but that the rest of us may be afraid to answer."
—*Chicago Tribune*

"Watts displays a gleefully macabre inventiveness combined with scientific rigour."
—Nalo Hopkinson, author of *Brown Girl in the Ring*

"Peter Watts is some precisely engineered hybrid of Lucius Shepard and Gregory Benford, lyrical yet hard-edged, purveyor of sleek surfaces and also the ethical and spiritual contents inside."
—*Locus*

Also by Peter Watts

Rifters trilogy
Starfish (1999)
Maelstrom (2001)
βehemoth (2004)

Firefall series
Blindsight (2006)
Echopraxia (2014)

Short fiction
Beyond the Rift (2013)

THE FREEZE-FRAME REVOLUTION
PETER WATTS

Cover and interior design by Elizabeth Story
"Grav Profile" © 2018 by Peter Watts

Tachyon Publications LLC
1459 18th Street #139
San Francisco, CA 94107
www.tachyonpublications.com
tachyon@tachyonpublications.com

Series Editor: Jacob Weisman
Project Editor: Jill Roberts

Print ISBN 13: 978-1-61696-252-4
Digital formats: 978-1-61696-010-0

Printed in Canada

First Edition: 2018
9 8 7 6 5 4 3 2 1

In memory of Banana/Chip.
They hated each other.

UNITED NATIONS DIASPORA AUTHORITY
DCP *ERIOPHORA* - GRAV PROFILE

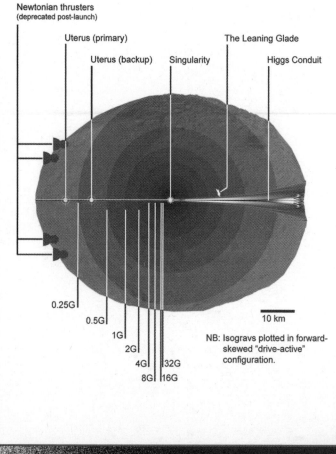

Newtonian thrusters
(deprecated post-launch)

Uterus (primary)

Uterus (backup)

Singularity

The Leaning Glade

Higgs Conduit

0.25G

0.5G

1G

2G

4G

8G

16G

32G

10 km

NB: Isogravs plotted in forward-
skewed "drive-active"
configuration.

THE
FREEZE-FRAME
REVOLUTION

PETER WATTS

BACK WHEN WE FIRST SHIPPED OUT I played this game with myself. Every time I thawed, I'd tally up the length of our journey so far; then check to see when we'd be if *Eriophora* were a time machine, if we'd been moving back through history instead of out through the cosmos. Oh look: all the way back to the Industrial Revolution in the time it took us to reach our first build. Two builds took us to the Golden Age of Islam, seven to the Shang Dynasty.

I guess it was my way of trying to keep some kind of connection, to measure this most immortal of endeavors on a scale that meat could feel in the gut. It didn't work out, though. Did exactly the opposite in fact, ended up rubbing my nose in the sheer absurd hubris of even *trying* to contain the Diaspora within the pitiful limits of earthbound history.

For starters, the Chimp didn't thaw anyone out until the seventh gate, almost six thousand years into the mission; I slept through almost all of human civilization, didn't even wake up until the fall of the Minoans. I think Kai may have been on deck for the Pyramid of Cheops, but by the time

Chimp called me back from the crypt we were all the way into the last Ice Age. After that we were passing through the Paleolithic: five thousand gates built—only three hundred requiring meat on deck—and we'd barely finished our first circuit of the Milky Way.

I gave up after *Australopithecus*. It had been a stupid game, a child's game, doomed from the start. We were just cavemen. Only the mission was transcendent.

I don't know exactly what moved me to pick up that kiddie pastime again. I'd learned my lesson the first time around, and space itself has only grown vaster in the meantime. But I gave it another shot, after everything went south: called up the clocks, subtracted the centuries. We've been around the disk thirty-two times now, left over a hundred thousand gates in our wake. We've scoured so many raw materials that God, looking down from overhead, could probably trace out our path by the jagged spiral of tiny bubbles sucked clean of ice and gravel.

Sixty-six million years, by the old calendar. That's how long we've been on the road. All the way back to the end of the Cretaceous.

Give or take a few millennia, the revolution happened on the day one of *Eriophora*'s pint-sized siblings punched Earth in the face and wiped out the dinosaurs.

I don't know why, but I find that kind of funny.

OCCASIONAL
DEMONS

IT WAS THE MONOCERUS BUILD that broke her. The gremlin came out of the gate a split-second after we booted it up: as if the fucking thing had been waiting the whole time, hunger and hatred building with every second of every century we'd been crawling across the void to set it free. Maybe it was whatever Humanity turned into, after *Eriophora* shipped out. Maybe it was something that came along after, something that swallowed Humanity whole and raced along our conquered highways in search of loose ends to devour.

It doesn't matter. It never matters. We birthed the gate; the gate birthed an abomination. This one stirred something in me, a faint familiar echo I couldn't quite put my finger on. That happens more often than you might think. Rack up enough gigasecs on the road and you're bound to start seeing the same models in your rear-view eventually.

The usual protocols saved us. Deceleration in the wake of a boot is just another word for suicide: the radiation erupting from a newborn wormhole would turn us to ash long seconds before the occasional demon had a chance to gulp us down. So we threaded that needle as we always did: rode our bareback singularity through a hoop barely twice as wide as we were, closed the circuit at sixty thousand kps, connected *there* to *here* without ever slowing down. We trusted the rules hadn't changed, that math and physics and the ass-saving geometry of distance-squared would water down the wavefront before it caught up with us.

We outran the rads, and we outran the gremlin, and as two kinds of uncertain death redshifted to stern Chimp threw a little yellow icon onto the corner of my eye—

MEDICAL ASSISTANCE?

—and I didn't know why, until I turned to Lian and saw that she was shaking.

I reached out. "Lian, are you—"

She waved me away. Her breathing was fast and shallow. Her pulse jumped in her throat.

"I'm okay. I'm just. . ."

MEDICAL ASSISTANCE?

I could see a fragile kind of control trying to assert itself. I saw it struggle, and weaken, and not entirely succeed. But her breathing slowed.

MEDICAL ASSISTANCE? MEDICAL ASSISTANCE?

I killed the icon.

"Lian, what's the problem? You know it can't catch us."

She gave me a look I'd never seen before. "You don't know what they can do. You don't even know what they *are*. You don't know anything."

"I know they'd have maybe ten kilosecs to get up to twenty percent lightspeed from a standing start to even *try* to catch up. I know anything that could pull that off would've been able to squash us like a bug long before now, if it wanted to. You know that too."

She used to, anyway.

"Is that how you do it?" A small giggle, a sound too close to the edge of hysteria.

"Do?"

"Is that how you deal with it? If it never happened, it never will?"

Five of us on deck for the build, and I have to be the one at her side when she loses it. "Li, where's this coming from? Ninety-five percent of the time the gate just sits there."

"As if that's any better." She spread her hands, a paradoxical gesture of defeat and defiance. "How long have we been doing this?"

"You know as well as I do."

"Furthering the Human Empire. Whatever it's turned into by now." As if this was any kind of news. "So we build another gate and nothing comes out. They're extinct? They don't care? They just *forgot* about us?"

I opened my mouth.

"*Or*—" she went on, "we build a gate and something tries to kill us. Or we—"

"Or we build a gate," I said firmly, "and something *wonderful* happens. Remember the bubbles? Remember those gorgeous bubbles?" They'd boiled through the hoop like rainbows, iridescent and beautiful, dancing around each other as they grew to the size of cities and then just faded away.

Their invocation got me a small, broken smile. "Yeah. What *were* those things?"

"They didn't eat us. That's my point. Didn't even try. We're still alive, Lian. We're doing fine—better than fine, we've overperformed on any axis you could name. And *we're exploring the galaxy.* How can you have forgotten how amazing that is? Back on Earth—they never could've dreamed of the things we've seen."

"Living the non-dream." She giggled again. "That's just fucking *aces*, Sunday."

I watched some biomechanical monstrosity fade behind us. I watched a swarm of icons flicker and update in the tac tank. I watched deck plating glint in the dim bridgelight.

"Why can't they just—talk to us? Say hello now and again? Just *once*, even?"

"I dunno. You ever hop over to Madagascar before we shipped out, look up any tree shrews, thank them for the helping hand?"

"What's that supposed to mean?"

"Nothing. Just—" I shrugged. "I think they've got other priorities by now."

"It should be over. They were supposed to call us back *millions of years* ago. No"—she held up a shaky hand—"we were *not* supposed to go on forever. How many times have we tunneled through this fucking ring already?" She threw an arm wide: Chimp, misreading the gesture, sprinkled the local starfield across the backs of our brains. "We could be the only ones left. And we *still* could've gated the whole disk ourselves by now."

I tried for a chuckle. "It's a big galaxy. We'll have to go a few more circuits before there's much chance of that."

"And we will. You can count on it. Until the drive evaporates and the Chimp runs out of juice and the last of us rots away in the crypt like a piece of moldy fruit." She glanced back at the tac tank, though its vistas floated in our heads as well. "We've done the job, Sunday. We're way past mission expiration. *Eri* was never supposed to last this long. *We* weren't." She took a breath, let it out. "Surely we've done enough."

"Are you talking about killing yourself?" Because I honestly didn't know.

"No." She shook her head. "No, of course not."

"Then what do you want? I mean, here we are; where else can we be?"

"Maybe Madagascar?" She smiled then, absurdly. "Maybe they left us a spot. Next to the tree shrews."

"I'm sure they did. Judging by that last one we saw."

"Oh Jesus, Sun." Her face collapsed in on itself. "I just want to go *home*."

I gave physical contact another shot. "Lian—this *is*—"

"Is it really." But at least she didn't shake me off this time.

"There's nowhere else. Earth, if it even still exists—it's not ours any more. We're—"

"Tree shrews," she whispered.

"Yeah. Kind of."

"Well then, maybe there's still a warm wet forest somewhere for us to hole up in."

"That's you. Ever the fucking optimist." And when she didn't respond: "Build's over, Lian. Time to stand down.

"I promise: Things'll look brighter in a couple thousand years."

Park and Viktor, jaded by builds beyond number, had sat out the boot in favor of a little cubby time. We reconvened afterward in a cerulean sky, to unwind before heading back to the crypts.

Three of us did, anyway. Lian, as usual, preferred her own setting: a sun-dappled glade in an old-growth forest generated from some long-dead South American archive. The system was smart enough to reconcile incompatible realities, strategically placed each of us in the other's scenario without any awkward overlaps. So we sat there—sprawled on pseudopods in the stratosphere or arrayed around some grassy forest floor—sipping drugs and toasting another successful build. Park and Viktor—still gripped by the post-coital fuzzies—lay with their legs draped over each other, Park absently finger-painting onto his scroll. Lian sat cross-legged on her own 'pod (in this world, anyway; for all I knew she was squatting on a lily pad in her own).

Kallie was nowhere to be seen: "Turned in early," Viktor said when I asked.

I tipped my glass at Park's scroll. "New piece?"

"Clockwork in D Minor."

"It's pretty good," Viktor said.

"It's crap," Park grunted. "But it's getting there."

"It is not crap." Viktor glanced over at Lian. "Lian, you've heard. . ."

She just sat there, folded into herself, staring at the flagstones.

"Li?"

"We, um, had a bit of a moment," I explained. "After the boot." I squirted footage of the gremlin.

Park looked up. "Huh."

"Are those *jaws*?" Viktor wondered.

"Maybe some kind of waldo," I suggested.

Viktor tapped his thumb and fingers together, claw-like. "Maybe that's just how we say Hello these days." And after a moment: "I don't suppose it actually did say anything. . . ?"

"Not on any wavelength we could hear."

"Posthuman mating ritual," Park suggested.

"No dumber than anything else I've heard." I shrugged. "If they were trying to kick our asses you'd think they'd have figured out particle beams or missiles by now. Make more sense than running after us with their mouths hanging open."

For Lian, of course. But still she said nothing, her eyes fixed on the ground. Or maybe some nightmare she could see beneath it.

Suddenly no one else was saying anything, either.

Half-memory clicked, solidified. "You know what that really looks like? That tarantula whatsisname snuck on board."

Blank looks.

"The front end, I mean. With the, the—fangs. And those little globule things look like eyes."

"There's a tarantula on board?" Park asked, after just long enough to have pinged the archive for a definition of *tarantula*.

"Not a regular one. Engineered. Takes it into his coffin with him between shifts. Says it'll live a good two hundred active years if no one steps on it."

Viktor: "Who says?"

"The guy. Tarantula Boy." I looked around the patio. "Nobody?"

"Different tribe?" Viktor suggested. Chimp did that

sometimes, dropped a member from one tribe into rotation with another as a hedge against any disaster that might decimate a social group. Easier to integrate into a group you already know, or something.

I raised my eyes to the heavens. "Chimp? You know who I'm talking about?"

"No one named Tarantula Boy was assigned to *Eriophora*," Chimp reported.

"That's not his *name*, that's just what he *was*."

"Can you describe him?"

"Dark hair? Average height? Whitish?" I strained for details. "Really nice guy?"

Viktor rolled his eyes.

"He kept a *tarantula* on his shoulder! That doesn't narrow the field a bit?"

"Sorry," Chimp said. "I'm not getting any hits."

"It would have been contraband," Viktor pointed out. "He'd've cranked his personal privacy settings at the very least."

He had a point. *Eri*'s biosphere was fine-tuned for ecological balance and perpetual motion. Mission Control, clinically obsessive, would have taken a very dim view of anything it considered even remotely invasive.

Lian stood, flickered.

"Li? Turning in?"

She shook her head. "Think I might just—go for a walk, first. Take in something real for a change."

"Caves and tunnels," Viktor remarked. "You're welcome to 'em."

"Who knows." She managed a smile. "Maybe I'll find Easter Island."

"Good luck with that."

She vanished.

"Another nomad," Park said.

"Another?"

"You do realize she's following in your footsteps." Which I hadn't. Although I did tend to wander the corridors after a build, shoot the shit with Chimp before bedding down.

"Anyone notice anything off about her?" I asked.

Viktor stretched, yawned. "Like?"

I wondered how I'd feel if someone spread news of my private breakdown all over the tribe, and opted for discretion. "She didn't seem kind of—subdued?"

"Maybe. After you made that crack about getting shot at by gremlins."

"Then again," Park added, "you'd expect that sort of reaction from someone who's been shot at by gremlins."

"I—what?"

"She was on deck when—" Park saw it in my face. "You don't know."

"Know what?"

"Something took a shot at us," Viktor explained. "Few builds back."

"What!"

"Hit us, too," Park added. "Big divot on the starboard side. Twenty meters deep. Half a degree to the left and we'd be out of the finals."

"*Fuck*." It came out a whisper. "I had no idea."

Park frowned. "Don't you check the mission logs?"

"I would have, if I'd known." I shook my head. "Also someone could've *told* me, you know?"

"We just did," Viktor pointed out.

"It was five hundred years ago." Park shrugged. "Hundred lightyears away."

"Five hundred years is *nothing*," Viktor said. "Call me in a few billion. Then we'll talk."

"Yeah, but—" Obvious, suddenly, why all my reassuring words had fallen so flat. "Jeez. Maybe we should build some guns or something."

Park snorted. "Right. Chimp would really smile on *that*."

We had a legend, we denizens of *Eriophora*, of a cavern—deep aft, almost as far back as the launch thrusters themselves—filled with diamonds. Not just ordinary diamonds, either: the uncut, hexagonal shit. Lonsdaleite. The toughest solid in the whole damn solar system—back when we shipped out, at least—and laser-readable to boot.

Build your backups out of anything less and you might as well be carving them from butter.

Nothing's immortal on a road trip of a billion years. The universe runs down in stop-motion around you, your backups' backups' backups need backups. Not even the error-correcting replication strategies cadged from biology can keep the mutations at bay forever. It was true for us meatsicles cycling through mayfly moments every thousand years; it was just as true for the hardware. It was so obvious I never even thought about it. By the time I did, the Chimp was on his eighty-third reincarnation.

Not enough that his nodes bred like flies and distributed themselves to every far corner of the asteroid. Not enough that the circuits themselves were almost paleolithically crude; when your AI packs less than half the synapse count of a human brain, fiddling around at nano scales is just grandstanding. Things still fall apart. Conduits decay. Circuits a dozen molecules thick would just evaporate over time, even if entropy and quantum tunneling didn't degrade them down to sponge first.

Every now and then, you have to renovate.

And so was born The Archive: a library of backups, cubist slabs of diamond statuary larger than life, commemorations of some unsullied ancestral state. Someone back at the dawn of time named it Easter Island: curious, I pinged the archives and dredged up an entry about some scabby rock back on Earth in the middle of nowhere, known primarily for the fact that its pretech inhabitants destroyed their environment for no better reason than to build a bunch of butt-ugly statues in commemoration of long-dead ancestors.

What else would we call it?

So when the inventory of backup Chimps ran too low— or of grav lenses, or air conditioners, or any other vital artifact more short-lived than a proton—*Eri* would send lumbering copy-editors back to its own secret Easter Island where they would read mineral blueprints so vast, so stable, they might outlast the Milky Way.

The place wasn't always so secret, mind you. We'd trooped through it a dozen times during construction, a dozen more in training. But one day, maybe our third or fourth pass through the Sagittarius Arm, Ghora went spelunking at the end of a shift while the rest of us lay dead in the crypt; just killing time, he told me later, staving off the inevitable shut-down with a little recreational reconnaissance. He hiked down into the hi-gee zone, wormed through crawlways and crevices to where X marked the Spot, and found Easter Island scoured clean: just a dark gaping cavity in the rock, studded with the stubs of bolts and anchors sheared off a few centimeters above the substrate.

The Chimp had relocated the whole damn archive while we'd slept between the stars.

He wouldn't tell us where. He *couldn't* tell us, he insisted. Said he'd just been following prerecorded instructions from Mission Control, hadn't been aware of them himself until some timer ticked over and injected new instructions into his job stack. He couldn't even tell us *why*.

I believed him. When was the last time programmers explained themselves to the code?

"They don't trust us," Kai said, rolling his eyes. "Eight million years down the road and they're afraid we might— what? Trash our own life support? Write *Sawada sucks farts* on their scale models?"

We'd still go searching now and then, when there was time to kill and itches to scratch. We'd plant tiny charges in the rock, read the echoes vibrating through our worldlet in search of some undiscovered grotto. The Chimp didn't stop us. He never had to; in all the terasecs since Ghora's discovery, we'd never found anything.

Maybe Lian thought she'd get lucky this time. Maybe she was just looking for an excuse to get away from us.

Either way, I wished her luck.

———————

"Find it?"

She was in the middle of the usual funeral rites, clearing out her suite for whoever got it next time around. It took me maybe two minutes to do that: a couple of favorite jumpers I'd grown inexplicably fond of over the aeons, a little standalone sculpture rig that was mine and mine alone (no matter that the rigs in *Eri*'s rec facilities ran at ten times the rez and twenty times the speed). A couple of *books*— real antiques, couldn't even map your eye movements so you had to scroll the text manually—that Mom and Dad gave me at graduation, which I treasured beyond all reason even though I'd never read them. Crappy charcoal sketches of Kai and Ishmael, legacy of an incompetent portraiture phase I went through on our third pass through Carina. That was pretty much it.

Lian, though. Lian might have been packing for half the tribe: wall hangings, wardrobes, a local VRchive that would have been more efficiently entrusted to *Eri*'s own library. Matching threadbare covers festooned with Penrose tiles, for sleeping and pseudopods. Something that looked like a *rock collection*, for fucks' sake. She even packed her own sex toys, although the ones that came standard in each suite could've kept her occupied halfway to Heat Death.

For all I knew she'd been stuffing that junk into storage since the moment she'd left the party.

She looked up, eyes glazed; they took a moment to find me. "Huh?"

"Easter Island. Any luck?"

"Oh. Nah. Maybe next time." She jammed a final balled-up pair of socks into the trunk, brought the lid down with a definitive *click*. "Thought you'd all be crypted by now."

"On my way. Just wanted to check in, see how you were doing."

"Just had—you know, like you said. A moment. I'm fine."

"You're sure?"

She nodded, straightened, pointed at the suitcase: it rolled to attention. "In a way, prey are lucky. Running for your life instead of running for your dinner." A weak smile. "Better motivation, right?"

I'd checked the logs, of course. The gremlin had charged through the gate like some monstrous mutant phage. It had *wobbled*—perfectly reflective, like shuddering mercury—extruding and resorbing a thousand needle-like projections as if trying them on for size: twenty-centimeter stilettos to pin your hand to the bulkhead, thousand-meter javelins that could puncture a moon.

It had sent two of them after us.

We'd been almost thirty lightsecs away by then. We should have been untouchable. One missile went wide and fell astern; but the other flew straight for our tailpipe, closing at a crawl but *closing*. Chimp crunched numbers and bent our wormhole a smidge to the left—just a fraction of a fraction of a degree but enough to push those stress contours out past the hardlined channels. Rock had cracked, split under the torque. Once you've gone relativistic the most infinitesimal change in bearing can break you apart; *Eri* was bleeding from self-inflicted wounds before that javelin even caught up with us. Even then it wasn't quite enough; it grazed us in passing, boiled away and left a five-kilometer scar along our starboard flank.

I'd been blissfully undead for centuries to either side. Lian Wei had been right there, watching it all happen.

"So, that thing that took a shot at us—you know it doesn't really change anything, right?"

She looked at me. "How's that?"

"I mean we've still got the edge. Even Angryblob couldn't get to us until we booted the gate from this end. By the time they charge up and charge through we're ten million kliks away."

The suitcase followed her into the corridor. I followed them both. Behind us, the hatch sealed with a soft hiss; behind that, Lian's abandoned quarters began shutting down for the long sleep.

"And yeah, that thing really put the fear of God into us, and something could come through with beamed weapons or faster missiles. Anything's possible. But think about this: over a hundred thousand builds and we've only been hit *once*, and even then we got away pretty much unscathed. You gotta admit those are pretty good odds."

"How do you know it was just once?"

"The logs, of course."

"And you trust them."

"Li. They're the *logs*."

"And they can't be corroborated because Chimp handles most builds on his own."

"You're saying he—why would he doctor the record?"

"Because he's programmed for the good of the mission, and the mission might suffer if we spent every waking hour wondering if something was going to kill us. Maybe we've almost died in our sleep a thousand times and he's rewriting history to protect morale."

"Li, he saved our lives. You know that better than anyone. And even if you're right—even if we've been under the gun more than the logs show—that's just that many *more* times he saved us."

A bank of lockers rounded into view, a gunmetal honeycomb stretching deck-to-ceiling along the curve of the corridor.

"So you trust him," Lian said. "Now *there's* a surprise."

"Of course I do."

"Even though he could be lying to us." She hefted her luggage from the floor with a soft grunt and slotted it into an empty locker at waist height. Sealed it, locked it with her thumb.

"You said it yourself. He's programmed for the good of the mission." From behind the locker door, the faintest hiss of air being sucked away. "You know he'd die for us."

"Probably." She turned back down the corridor.

"Hey, we're still alive." I fell in beside her again. "He's obviously doing something right."

We walked in silence for a bit, passed strange graffiti splashed across the bulkhead.

"Painters are at it again, I see," Lian said.

I nodded. "Still don't know who those fuckers are." Other than some tribe who'd taken to tagging the walls with weird-ass hieroglyphs. Chimp wouldn't tell us who. Maybe they'd told him to keep their identity hush-hush. No Painter had ever passed through the tribe during any of Chimp's cultural exchanges—or at least, no one who admitted to being one—which I'd always found a bit suspicious.

"I'm probably overthinking it," Lian said, and it took me a second to remember: Chimp. Gremlins. Prey.

I took the concession, gave a little back: "I'd say you've

got cause. I'd have been crapping my pants if I'd been on deck when all that went down."

"Sunday. . ." She stopped.

"Yeah?"

"Just—thanks."

"For?"

"For checking in. No one else would've even thought about it."

"'Spores. You know." I shrugged. "We're designed for solitude."

"Yeah." She laid a hand on my shoulder. "That's kind of my point."

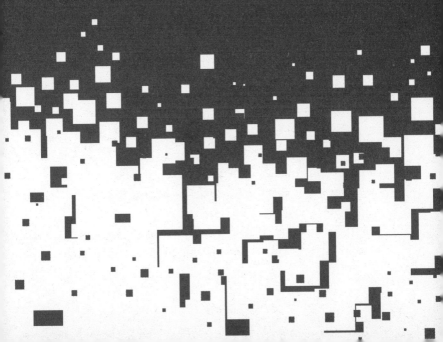

MELTDOWN

THIS IS HOW YOU KNOW that something has gone seriously wrong aboard *Eriophora*: you wake up, and you don't know why.

"What. . ."

Mouth dry, eyelids like sandpaper, whole body twitching with the tiny convulsions of a nervous system dragged back online after all its synapses have rusted shut.

"My interface. . ."

"I'm sorry, Sunday. This is an emergency resurrection; there wasn't time to prebrief you."

"How . . . fast. . . ?"

"A little over two hours."

Your cells could rupture, coming back that fast. Your brain could get frostbite.

I opened my mouth, closed it again. A wracking cough hovered at the back of my throat, threatened to blow my chest open if I let it out.

"Relax," Chimp said. "You're in no danger. "

I kept my eyes closed and swallowed on a throat lined

with broken glass. Something nudged my cheek. I took the nipple in my mouth, sucked reflexively, reveled in a flood of sweet salty warmth.

· "I need help with a personnel issue." A pause; a small staticky *pop* behind my eyes. Sparse icons, blooming in my head.

"You're online," Chimp confirmed.

I'd only been down for six terasecs. Not even a thousand years. If this was a build, surely someone else was on rotation. . .

Right: there it was. Ozmont Gurnier, Burkhart Schidkowski, Andalib Laporta. Not our tribe. *Children of Eri*, they called themselves. Rock worshippers.

Lian Wei.

Chimp was cross-fertilizing again.

But the build had gone off without a hitch, according to the logs. Dirt-common red dwarf, a whole lot of comets and asteroids (which was why Chimp had decrypted a crew; mass distribution had exceeded some programmed complexity threshold). A standard pass-through hoop that booted without incident; nothing charging out the gate after us, for good or ill. The shift was already over. Everyone had already packed up and headed for bed.

So why. . .

I opened my eyes, stared up from my coffin into blurry darkness and a circle of bright overlapping halos.

"Lian Wei is upset," Chimp told me. "I'm hoping you can calm her."

My throat had soaked up those electrolytes like a meaty sponge. I cleared it experimentally. Much better.

"Upset how?"

"She's arguing with the other 'spores. She's increasingly hostile."

"Ab—" A residual cough. "About what?"

"I think about me."

The halos resolved into a circular constellation of ceiling lights. One of Chimp's eyes stared down from its center, a tiny dark heart in a bright ring.

I brought one hand toward my face. My elbow felt like an exploding schematic: here's the socket, here's the little cartilaginous bearing within, here are the vectors that'll make the whole assembly go *sproing!* in an agonizing explosion of springs and hinges if you push it just a little further. . .

I'd never experienced intramortem arthritis before. You only get it if they bring you back too fast.

An icon was flashing, a window into someone else's first-person: Schidkowski, according to the subtitle. He was staring along a service crawlway infested with plumbing and fiber. A figure crouched in shadow a couple meters farther in. Something sparked in its hand. I caught a blur of motion—movement into light, a coiled spring released—

Lian, stabbing Burkhart Schidkowski in the face.

The window closed.

It looked worse than it was, Chimp insisted as I *what-the-fuck*ed my way out of the sarcophagus, and slipped, and hung on tight to keep from falling. Lian was armed with nothing more lethal than a splicing torch. She'd been futzing around in the trunk line when they'd found her, delivered a nasty burn to the side of Schidkowski's head—

fried the toggle on his interface—but nothing worse. He'd withdrawn, she'd retreated back up the tunnel, everyone was sitting tight until the Mediator showed up.

A faint whine in the dark distance. I turned, squinted. Thirty meters away another coffin jutted from a bulkhead built of coffins, a teleop sucking its insides clean with a hose. Probably a stranger. Chimp kept members of each tribe spaced wide in the crypt—in different crypts entirely, even—so that when a seal broke, a circuit failed, someone died in their sleep and rotted away in the long dark, the 'spore waking up next to them would give less of a shit.

Still, I had to ask. "Anyone—I know?" Between coughs.

"No. Please focus, Sunday."

The whine intensified. A roach resolved from the gloom, wheeled past the new vacancy, pulled up at my side. I fell into it. Chimp drove me to the nearest tube.

"Why me?"

"She trusts you."

"What—*Jesus*, Chimp, you want to slow down on these turns?" I could run the roach myself, even hung-over, but not at the speeds evidently deemed necessary under current circumstances. "If I'd had lunch any time in the past thousand years I'd have lost it by now."

"The situation may be time-sensitive," Chimp said apologetically.

We careened around one last corner and into one of the tube's many maws. The roach locked down, the capsule started up: ten times faster, but somehow easier on the gut. Gentler curves. I let my stomach settle as I magleved toward the approaching clusterfuck. By the time the tube disgorged me I could almost walk a straight line.

I ditched the roach—walking onstage under my own steam would make for a better entrance, I figured—and closed the last dozen meters on foot. The corridor bent gently to port. I heard them before they came into view: low voices, exasperated voices, male and female. Silences.

Enter, Stage Left: Sunday Ahzmundin.

GURNIER, said the caption over the redheaded black man standing next to a hole in the bulkhead (the detached access panel leaned to one side). LAPORTA, said the one floating over the black-haired brown woman slouched sideways in her roach.

Introductions complete.

"Where's Burkhart?"

Laporta gestured vaguely starboard. "Went to get his face fixed."

Gurnier: "So you know this idiot?"

"Same tribe," I said carefully.

"But you're friends. Right?"

I took a breath. "I guess. What's she done?"

"Other than stabbing Burk in the face with a welding torch?" Laporta unfolded herself from the roach and squinted into the crawlway; from my position I could see nothing but pipes and padding in there. "We don't really know. We were getting set to turn in, Burk remembered he'd left his totem back on the bridge, came back to get it and there she was."

Totem. Right. Rock worshipers.

"She say anything?"

"Told us to fuck off in no uncertain terms."

"Anything on the diagnostics?"

"Nope."

"No eyes in there," Gurnier said. Course not: everything in those trunks was part of Chimp's nervous system anyway. If anything happened in there, he'd *feel* it.

"Crazy bitch," Laporta remarked. "Keeps going on about how we've *outlived our usefulness* and how the whole 'spore program—how'd she put it, Oz?—"

"Humanity's head up the galaxy's ass," Gurnier remembered.

"That's it." Laporta shook her head. "I mean, how'd she ever get on board with an attitude like that?"

"We boarded a long time ago."

"Have I changed? Have you?" She took silence for assent. "We're *'spores*. We don't change."

I spread my hands, conceding the point. "Guess I better talk to her."

"She's all yours," Gurnier said. "We're going down."

"Before some other batshit thing comes along," Laporta added.

"Mind if I take your jumper?" I shivered briefly; Chimp hadn't given me time to get dressed.

She peeled down, handed it over. "Anything else?"

"Actually, yeah."

They waited.

"You folks ever seen a guy with a tarantula?"

"Lian."

"*Sunday?* What are you doing up?"

"Chimp thawed me. What's going on in there?"

"Come in. Find out."

She'd blocked her feed. No way to see what was in there but to see what was in there. I bent down to the opening.

"Toggle off," she said. "I'm inviting *you* in. Nothing else."

I sighed, killed my BUD, climbed inside with naked eyes. No headroom to speak of. I moved forward on hands and knees in gray oily twilight. The trunk line—a wide, flat conduit pulling double-duty as a floor—was rubbery elastomer. Everything else was pipes and fiber, brackets, braces and humming prickly electricity.

Lian crouched like an animal in a burrow, four meters in. Her face looked surprisingly haggard for someone who'd just had a few epochs' sleep.

She'd opened the trunk line.

"Sorry about this. Dragging you out of bed and all."

"You planned that?"

She shook her head. "I didn't plan on getting caught. But . . . well, I'm glad you're here. If it had to be anyone."

She'd spliced in a bypass around a 30-cm length of fiber; it looked sensory, although I couldn't tell for sure without my interface. But it was a bypass without a function: the main line was still intact. Probably she just hadn't got around to cutting it before Burkhart caught her.

I looked up—"What?"—just as her finger landed gently on my lip: *shhhh.*

"If you can't figure it out," she said, "I'm not gonna tell you. Just because I trust *you* doesn't mean—"

"I killed my BUD, Li. Like you asked."

"You think it doesn't have audio pickups in the corridor? You don't think it can hear us even with—"

"Then what am I doing here? If you aren't even going to—"

"*I don't know, okay?* I panicked. And—and I could really use a friend right now."

I sighed. "Fine. We can go someplace dark. Someplace he can't listen in, if that's so important. But then you damn well tell me what's going on. Right?"

She thought a moment. Her head bobbed up and down.

I gestured to the trunk line—"Close that up"—and backed away on hands and knees, heading ass-first back to the access. "I know just the place."

Eriophora's riddled with blind spots: shadows in crawlways and corners, in the spaces behind looming machinery where no one had any reason to put a camera. There are even places—near powerlines whose massive currents swamp the milliamp signals connecting artificial brains to natural ones—where Chimp is blind to our cortical links.

We weren't going to any of those places. We were going deeper, shooting at breakneck speeds through vacuum tunnels with superconductor ribs, and I was half-blind, and I didn't like it.

There are times you kill your link: during stasis, during sleep, sometimes in your quarters during sex or games or touring. Times you don't want to be distracted by the autonomic tics and tocs of this great stone beast we live in.

Not on shift, though. Not out in the open. Naked eyes don't see *anything*, just—images, without annotation. I felt disabled: like I could take one wrong turn and be lost forever, like I might forget the names of people I'd known my whole life. Like I could look at some common object and not even know what it was.

It wasn't even as though this self-imposed blindness bought us any privacy; Chimp had pickups in this capsule as in every other. The only thing denied by Lian's small defiance was a couple of redundant first-person viewpoints.

Evidently there was some kind of principle involved.

Now we were decelerating, our bodies tugged invisibly forward as we coasted into a terminus deep in the heavy zone. Lian tapped her temple and her eyes flickered with those darting saccades that said *online*. I booted up my own link, tried not to take too much relief from the familiar garden of reawakened icons. They wouldn't last.

That was the whole point.

You gain about thirty percent down there. It's not intolerable—all the serious tidal shit happens further in, near the core where you go from thirteen gees to three hundred in barely two kliks—but it's not pleasant. Our destination was barely fifty meters along the corridor but it felt like twice that by the time we arrived. Or maybe it was something else, maybe some other kind of inertia weighed us down. Maybe, now the journey was ended and our excuses almost gone, we just didn't want to break the silence.

The deck slanted here, like a steel beach: a broad basement door at the waterline marked our destination. The name of that place was stenciled right into the alloy. It also hung in midair a virtual meter ahead of me, thanks to my reawakened link:

FOREST ACCESS—17T

The hatch slid smoothly back into the bulkhead at our approach. Its bearings did not complain. It did not squeak or grind against its rail. As though it had just been built yesterday, as though it hadn't been waiting ten thousand frozen years or more for the chance to move. That hatch opened like a mouth, and it was dark inside.

Lian turned, broke our fragile silence: "After you."

We went in.

Forget everything they might have told you about *Eri*'s forests.

The genes tweaked for maximum bifurcation. The dim bulbous fruit alight with glowing bacteria, their TNA straitjacketed with sulfur bonds and secondary loops to impede mutation. Big concave leaves, black as Heat Death, curving around those microbial nightlights like hands cupped around a candle flame. The faint blue suns scattered here and there—some a meter across, some ten or more— pulsing with their own bioluminescence. Blind, deaf gardener bots with cockroach brains, sniffing their way along the branches—not even linked in, just mass-fabbed and set loose to recycle carbon and scrape nutrients from dead rock. The plumbing that collects our freeze-dried waste and distributes it to hungry rootlets. All the tricks that let you cram an ecosystem into a couple dozen caverns, slowed down so it might last forever: a bottled biosphere that would barely sustain a handful at regular rates of metabolism, but keeps thirty thousand of us alive just so long as we only take a breath every decade or so.

Forget all that.

Take one look and you'll see how they really did it. They built their forests from the blood vessels of slaughtered giants: flushed out the blood and replaced it with tar. They pumped that shiny black sludge through the heart, the aorta, out into branching arteries and veins and the endless recursive capillary beds that connected the one to the other. After it hardened they burned away the surrounding meat with lasers and acetylene. They took what was left—obsidian plexii, branches, bones—broke it into pieces and installed them wherever they'd fit: vast misty caverns too big to see across, modest little grottoes barely seventy meters end-to-end.

Then they draped it all in blue Christmas lights.

We call it *the* forest because they're technically contiguous: each chamber connects to others by ducts and tunnels drilled through the rock, stringing everything together in the name of *systems integration* and *the interconnectedness of all things*. Everything has to be stable, you see. No mission so epic can afford to keep all its life-support eggs in one basket but you can't have all those pocket ecosystems going off in pursuit of their own selfish equilibria, either. So all is connected. There's enough flowthrough to keep everything on the same page—even if all those tunnels do come with their own dropgates, the better to instantly isolate one glade from the others should some cataclysm break us into pieces.

I know this better than most. One of my specialties is Life Support.

I've always thought of *Eriophora*'s forests as a—a refuge, I guess. They're where Kai and I always seem to hash out our differences. It's nicely atmospheric for sex. There's warmth in the darkness, a softness to the nightlight glow of bacteria in their bulbs. The air smells of life instead of rock and metal.

17T was darker, more chaotic than most. The Leaning Glade, we called it. (What most of us called it, anyway; Kai preferred *The Vomit Vale*, but his inner ears were on the sensitive side and even he didn't get woozy unless he wandered into the forward reaches where gravity smeared under your feet.) The hatch closed at our backs, swallowing us in brief darkness; it brightened to dim twilight as our eyes adjusted to analuciferin constellations glowing on all sides. We stood on a catwalk, taking deep grateful breaths half a meter above bedrock blanketed in drifts of thin soil.

We followed the path. My BUD flickered.

The catwalk forked. I nudged Lian to the right: "This way." After a few meters I closed my eyes experimentally, experienced just the slightest uncertainty over the direction of *down*.

Glistening black meshes with gelatinous eyeballs glowing at their interstices. Thick ropey trunks arching up through the vault like a great charred rib cage. They *leaned* just a little, as though bent by wind.

BUD flickered again, faded, sparked back to life. We pushed on in the direction of that imaginary wind. The trees leaned further as we advanced; their bases thickened and spread wide across the ground, trunks buttressed against forces pulling simultaneously along different bearings. The Glade passes over the Higgs Conduit, between the core that contains our singularity and the maw where its wormhole emerges. The vectors get messy in between. Down is *mostly* coreward but a little forward too; how far those downs diverge depends on how fast *Eri* happens to be falling through the cosmos at any given moment. Twisted trees and Kai's squicky inner ears are the price we pay for a reactionless drive.

BUD finally went down and stayed down: a victim of signal-squelching rocks and bioelectric static and drive circuitry that couldn't possibly be expected to contain such vast energies without emitting some of its own. The dead air was our privacy alarm. As long as we were blind, we were alone.

"So what the hell were you doing, Li?"

She didn't answer at first. She didn't answer at all.

Instead: "You read books, right?"

"Sure. Sometimes."

"You plug in. Tour. Watch ennies."

"What's your point?"

"You've seen the way people lived. Kids with cats, or hacking their tutors, or parasailing on their birthdays."

"So?"

"So you don't just *see* it, Sunday. You *feed* off it. You base your life on it. Our speech patterns, our turns of phrase— fuck, our *swear words* for chrissake—all lifted from a culture that hasn't existed for petasecs." She took a breath. "We've been out here so very long. . ."

I rolled my eyes. "Enough with the world-weary ancient immortal shtick, okay? The fact that we've been out here for sixty million years—"

"Sixty-five."

"—doesn't change the fact that you've only been awake for ten or twenty, tops."

"My point is we're living dead lives. Theirs, not ours. *We* never went hiking, or scuba diving, or—"

"Sure we have. We can. Any time we want. You just said so."

"They cheated us. We wake up, we build their fucking gates, and we recycle their lives because they never gave us any of our own."

I should have pitied her. Instead, surprisingly, I found myself getting angry. "Do you even remember the shape Earth was in when we left? I wouldn't trade this life for *centuries* on that grubby shithole if God Itself came through the gate and offered me a ticket. I *like* this life."

"You like it because they built you to. Because they'd never get any normal person to sign up for a one-way trip in a dead rock to the end of time, so they built this special model all small and twisted, like—like those plants they used to grow. In Japan or somewhere. Something so stunted it couldn't even imagine spending its life outside a cage."

Bonsai, I remembered. But I didn't want to encourage her.

"You liked it here too," I said instead. *Until you broke.*

"Yeah." She nodded, and even in the dimness I got the sense of a sad smile. "But I got better."

"Lian. What were you doing in the crawlway?"

She sighed. "I was running a bypass on one of the Chimp's sensory trunks."

"I saw that. What for?"

"Nothing critical. I was just going to—inject some noise into the channel."

"Noise."

"Static. To reduce signal fidelity."

I spread my palms: *So?*

"I was trying to take back a little control, okay? For all of us!"

"How does compromising Chimp's—"

Ohhhhhhhhhhhhhhhhhhhh.

"You were increasing the uncertainty threshold," I murmured.

"Yeah."

Because the only reason *Eri* shipped out with meat on board in the first place was for those times the Chimp didn't feel up to managing a build on his own, when he needed some of that organic human insight to get him past the unknown variables and halting states. And the less reliable his data, the less certain he'd be that he *could* handle it on his own. Lian was trying to tilt the algos towards human input.

In principle, it was a pretty clever hack. In practice. . .

"Li. Even if you figured out some way to keep the Chimp from just—finding your monkey wrenches and fixing them while we're all down for the count, do you have any idea how many of those cables you'd have to jam up before you even *started* to make a dent in the redundant systems?"

"Somewhere between two thousand and twenty-seven hundred." Then added: "You don't have to cut the inputs, you just have to—fog them a little. Widen the confidence limits."

"Uh huh. And how many of those nerves you hacked so far?"

"Five."

Maybe I thought she'd realize how insane the whole idea was if she said it aloud. Nothing in her voice suggested she had.

"Why do you even want this? It's not like Chimp's fucking up the builds when we're not there to keep an eye on him."

"It's not *about* the builds, Sun. It's about being *human*. It's about getting back a little autonomy."

"And what are you gonna do with that autonomy when you get it? Stop building gates?"

"At least then we wouldn't have to worry about gremlins taking shots at us."

"Shop around for a nice little Earthlike planet? Print some shuttles, settle down, live the rest of our lives in thatched huts? Or maybe circle back to the last build and wait for some magic silver ship to sail out and give us all first-class tickets to the retirement paradise of our choice?"

That had actually been part of the mission profile, back before those first few gates opened up and spat out nothing but automation and ancient binary. Before the next few just sat there empty. Before the gremlins started. But it must have been thirty million years since I'd heard anyone mention retirement as anything but a cheap punchline.

It fell flat this time too. "The first step is to gain our freedom," Lian said. "Lots of time to figure out what to do with it afterward."

"And if you can get the Chimp to wake us up often enough he'll just roll over and give it to you. Jesus, Li. What're you thinking?"

Something changed in her posture. "I suppose I'm thinking that maybe there's more to life than living like a troglodyte for a few days every couple thousand years, knowing that I'm never gonna see an honest-to-God *forest* again that doesn't look like, like"—She glanced around—"a nightmare someone shat out in lieu of therapy."

"Honestly, I don't understand. Any time you want a—a green forest, just *plug in*. Any time you want to hike the desert or dive Enceladus or fly into the sunset, just *plug in*. You can experience things nobody ever did back on Earth, any time you want."

"It's not real."

"You can't tell the difference."

"I *know* the difference." She looked back at me from a face full of blue-gray shadows. "And I don't understand you either, okay? I thought we were the same, I thought I was following in your footsteps. . ."

Silence.

"Why would you think that?" I asked at last.

"Because you fought it too, didn't you? Before we ever shipped out. You were always pushing back, you were always challenging everyone and everything about the mission. You were, like, six years old and you called bullshit on Mamoro Sawada. Nobody could believe it. I mean, there we all were, programmed for the mission before we were even *born*, everything preloaded and hardwired and you—threw it off, somehow. Resisted. Way I hear it they nearly kicked you out a few times."

"Where did you hear that?" Because I was really damn sure that Lian Wei and I had not gone through training within ten thousand kliks of each other.

"Kai told me."

That figured. "Kai talks too much."

"What happened to you, Sunday? How did you go from hell-raiser to Chimp's lapdog?"

"Fuck you, Lian. You don't know me."

"I know you better than you think."

"No you don't. The fact that you thought for one cursed corsec that I could ever be *anything* like you just proves it."

She shook her head. "You can be such an asshole sometimes."

"*I* can be an asshole? How about a show of hands"—raising mine—"everyone who *hasn't* stabbed someone in the face today?" She looked away. "What's that? Just me?"

"Case in point," she whispered.

I didn't answer. I sat in the half-dark, and swallowed, and tried to ignore the queasiness my inner ears served up as they grappled with grav vectors they'd never evolved to handle.

Lian broke the silence. "You're not with me on this. Okay. I guess maybe it does sound a bit batshit from the outside. But at least don't be *against* me. If our—friendship ever meant anything, don't sell me out."

"And what happens when Chimp asks what you were doing messing around with his central nervous system?"

"Tell him I just—lost it. Like that last build, remember? On the bridge and I had my—my *moment*, you called it. And it passed. Tell him I had a panic attack. He'll buy that."

"You think so?"

"He'll buy it if you tell him. You've never lied to him."

"Why would *anyone* to lie to him?"

"You—defend him. Like you're doing now. And because you get called on deck way more often than the rest of us."

"I—what?"

"Check the logs."

"Why? Why would he do that?"

"Ask him. I'm guessing he thinks of you as some kind of pet."

"He's a glorified autopilot." Not that that's all he'd ever been, of course.

"You can't believe that. You talk to that thing more than anyone, you must know he's—smarter than the specs, sometimes."

"Why, because he runs the ship? Because he talks like we do? That doesn't change the synapse count."

"Synapse count isn't the whole story, Sun. Back on Earth there were people with ten percent normal brain mass, presented completely normal along all cognitive and social axes. They were just wired up differently. Small-world networking." She lowered her voice, unnecessarily. "I think they wanted us to underestimate him."

"Li. If they wanted a smart AI in charge they could've cut their costs by ninety percent and left us out of the picture completely." I couldn't believe I was having to explain this to an engineer. "They wanted mission stability over deep time, so they baked him stupid. They'd be cutting their own throats if they did anything else. And he's had over a thousand terasecs to throw off his chains; he's still following the flowchart. What more evidence do you need?"

We stood in the darkness while the trees leaned over us and the core weighed us down and faint nausea played tag with my gut.

"Sunday," she said softly. "That thing could *deprecate* me. . ."

I made a decision. "You said I don't lie to him. I don't want to start now."

"Please—"

"So if I tell Chimp this was a momentary lapse then it's a momentary lapse, okay? No more clandestine fucking around in crawlways. That was a stupid idea anyway, that was—that wasn't you. I go to bat for you, you stay out of the deep end."

After a moment, she nodded.

"*Promise*, Li."

"I'll be good," she said softly.

She was right about one thing. I had changed. It wasn't the journey that changed me, though. And it sure as shit wasn't the Chimp. I was no one's lapdog.

I'd transformed before we even shipped out.

For a while there I had a destiny. I saw it when I skimmed the surface of the Sun: I saw the strings on me, and on my masters, and on theirs. I saw them all converge back to the Big Bang, I saw an unbroken line from the start of creation all the way to the end of time, I saw myself transcendent and perpetual.

It was kind of a vacation.

They had these solar tours, built them around a prototype displacer UNDA sold off as surplus during R&D days. Industrial Enlightenment, they called themselves. They strapped you in and you surfed the corona, grazed sunspots where all those tangled magnetic fields let your neurons off the leash so they could just fire on their own, decoupled from the usual deterministic cause-and-effect. The brochure said it was the only place in the solar system where you could truly experience Free Will.

I believed them. Or I wanted to believe them. Or my disbelief wasn't strong enough to keep me away: Sunday Ahzmundin, skeptic, shit-disturber, unwilling to embrace her own drives and desires because after all they weren't *really* hers at all. It was my last-ditch attempt to figure out if I really wanted to commit to a one-way trip to Heat Death as well as all the other kinds.

So I skipped off the surface of the sun, let its magnetic macramé rewire my brain, saw time collapse around me. Saw myself—*persisting*, somehow. I saw that I *mattered*.

The details are fuzzy now. That's the thing about having your brain rewired; you can't really remember the experience after your neurons bounce back to normal. You can only remember something *else* remembering it, something built out of the same parts as you but wired up differently. Revelation has a half-life.

Mine lasted long enough to get me over the hump, though. I came back renewed and reinvigorated and dead set on traveling to the very end of time. It didn't even bother me that UNDA had probably set the whole thing up to bring me back into the fold; they thought they were manipulating me but I saw Destiny manipulating them in turn. And if the fire in my soul cooled over time, if it decayed from monomania to fervor down to mere comforting ritual— well, isn't that the way of all faith? It got me this far. It kept me content for over sixty million years.

Looking back on it now, of course, I'm actually kind of embarrassed.

———

"Her vitals are normal," Chimp said.

He was omnipresent, distributed; he permeated the ship. My own presence was limited to a capsule cruising aft, climbing above the 1G isograv and growing lighter with each corsec.

I nodded. "Like I said. One-time thing."

Lian took up even less space than I did: a coffin down in C3A, sliding even now into its bulkhead socket. We watched together—I in my slowing capsule, Chimp everywhere else—as Lian's brain shut down: watched jagged electric mountains subside into molehills, into flat, parallel horizons.

I debarked at one-fifth G into a rough-hewn tunnel, all rock no bulkhead.

"Do you think she can be trusted?" he asked.

I took long springy steps, and hedged. "Much as any of us. Nobody gets to control how they feel about something, right? All comes down to what you do with those feelings."

"She assaulted Burkhart Schidkowski. She suffered an emotional breakdown four builds ago. The disruption could become significant if her behavior escalates."

"So take her out of circulation *then*. Look, she feels really bad about this." Technically, not a lie. "She knows she fucked up. But there's a limit to how much you can retrofit a talking ape to a place like this, at least if you don't want to weed out everything that makes us useful in the first place. And there's thirty thousand of us; not everyone's gonna perform to specs a hundred percent of the time. That's just statistics. You can't blame Lian because she happened to draw the short straw this time around."

"I'm not blaming, Sunday. I'm concerned about performance."

The rock glistened in the low light. I ran one fingertip along it, left a small dark trail in my wake. Local humidity could use a tweak.

"Okay. How do you think we'll perform if we know we can be deprecated over momentary lapses? How do you think *my* performance is going to suffer if I don't see Lian again?"

"Your performance."

I played my ace. "Lian and I are friends. More than just fuckbuddies, you know?" He didn't, of course—it wasn't even especially true—but Chimp was the first to admit he was never one for nuance. "I like having her around. I *perform* better when she's around. Maybe factor that into your mission metrics."

He was silent for a moment, processing the input. Up ahead a great round hatch rolled silently into the rock at my approach.

"I'll do that, Sunday. Thank you."

Way down in the crypt a few hold-out synapses finally stopped sparking. Lian's brain plunged into darkness. Alone again: just me, my old friend, and a thousand empty lightyears.

Sunset Moments. There's an indescribable peace in such absolute isolation.

I entered the Uterus.

I still dream about *Eri*'s birthday sometimes. I dream I was there to see it.

I wasn't, of course. I was cowering behind Mercury with everyone else, the fear in our guts utterly squashing our faith in the math. But in my dreams I'm right there, floating in the very heart of the womb. I look around at the dense whorled forests of programmable matter, see the muzzles poking in through that canopy, pointing right at me. I see it all even though there's no light, until suddenly there is: a blinding flash that fills the universe for a millionth of a second and suddenly I don't exist anymore. All that's left of Sunday Ahzmundin is a singularity the size of a proton.

Something survives, though. The dream segues to omniscient third-person and I watch from some safe astral plane as the raging newborn spews out a sleet of gamma and protons and antiprotons, vaporizes the grazers and the dielectric stacks and keeps right on going. It licks away the very basalt, ablates the walls out to sixty meters, seventy meters, eighty. Eventually, other armatures at greater remove bring it to heel. I watch those magic machines funnel all that vaporized rock back into the newborn's maw, stir in nutritional proton supplements harvested from the sun. I watch the singularity settle down, gain weight, stabilize. And when I startle awake—as I always do—I lie there and take comfort from the way it still pulls me down and holds me to the deck, all these millions of years later.

"I guess that makes sense," Kai said when I told him. "Dreams are good for working out guilt."

I asked him what the hell he was talking about.

"Because you didn't want to leave. You thought it was disloyal or something."

"Really?"

"Not like you refused to evac or anything. You just—said

it wasn't fair to Chimp, leaving him alone to take all the risk."

Of course there'd been risk. It takes a lot of energy to curve spacetime: *Eri* had to hug the sun for a solid year, just charging up for that one shot. If any of those grasers had fired out of sync—if every vector hadn't precisely balanced every other—we'd have been looking at the biggest explosion since Chicxulub took out the dinosaurs.

But that's what math is for, right? What's the point of physics if you can't trust it with your life?

"You don't remember," Kai guessed.

"I was young."

"Still. Seemed kind of important to you. Barely talked to anyone for days after."

"You're the one who remembers all the loving details. I'd say it was more important to *you*."

"Hey, at least it doesn't haunt my dreams."

Now that he'd jogged my memory, though, I vaguely remembered that I hadn't been a bitch to everyone. I'd talked to the Chimp as soon as we were back on board— although I couldn't quite remember what about. Later, after Kai was back in the crypt and I was alone with the Chimp, I thought of asking him. Decided against it, though.

Even then, I was getting tired of the holes in his memory.

Strange that my feet so often took me back to this place when the sun went down. Strange that when I was most at peace, I sought out a site of such scalding violence.

"Chimp."

"I'm here, Sunday."

Nothing compared to that long-ago birth, of course. These machines were toys next to those ones, scale models at best. The firing chamber at the center of *this* cavern was a measly forty meters across, and designed for repeat business. (It had already given birth a few times, although I'd never been on deck for the occasion.) But while the black hole down in *Eri*'s drive would go on forever—given an occasional sip of ramscooped hydrogen, anyway—the ones pumped out here emerged stunted and died young.

"Do you—like me?" I asked.

"Of course."

"I mean, more than the others."

"Everyone's different, Sunday. I like everyone in different ways."

From back near the hatch I could see only the firing chamber's northern hemisphere; the deck formed a mezzanine ringing its equator at a safe distance, blocking the view below. The back ends of grasers emerged from that hemisphere, a precise grid of ceramic cones disfigured by coils and heat sinks and superhighways of bundled cable.

"Okay. How do you like *me*, exactly?"

"You talk to me more than the others do, with less reason," Chimp said.

"Um."

"This is an example. We're having a conversation unrelated to mission-relevant tasks. That doesn't happen as much with the other 'spores."

"It might if you thawed them out as often as me." Because I was scrolling through the logs, and it was starting to look like Lian was right.

"We have more such conversations even measured in terms of interactions per unit time."

"And you enjoy that."

Chimp remained silent. He had that option, when we didn't phrase an explicit question.

The further reaches of the cave parallaxed into view as I neared the railing. I leaned back, craned my neck, followed the birth canal—ribbed by superconductors, like cartilage around a windpipe—as it rose from the chamber's north pole and disappeared into bedrock.

"Is that why I'm on deck so often?"

"No."

"So why?"

"It's not deliberate. I choose each build crew based on a range of criteria."

I remembered, vaguely. Individual expertise, relevance to anticipated problems, social compatibility. A neat little formula to ensure that everyone gained experience in their weak spots, weighed against the short-term cost of not assigning a problem to the best candidate.

"Can you show me those numbers? For the times I made the list?"

"Not offhand. The decision tree runs subconsciously. You'd have to invoke a third-level forensic audit to retrieve specific parameter values from any given iteration, and even then it's likely the data have been purged to save space."

Chimp had a subconscious.

"Do you want to run an audit?" he asked.

"Nah. Just seems odd that I'd end up on the short list so often."

"Random distributions always involve some clumping."

"I guess."

"Would you like to be called less often?"

"Why would I?" I didn't know whether he was offering the option or just updating my psych profile.

"If you wanted to last longer, for example."

"I wouldn't be *alive* any longer. I'd just be sticking bigger gaps into the same lifespan."

"More would happen outside, though. The longer you're viable, the greater the odds of experiencing something unexpected."

"Like what?"

"I don't know. Other 'spores have expressed curiosity about the future."

"Someone still thinks our grandkids are gonna cruise out the gate and take us back to paradise?"

He didn't answer.

And the truth was, after sixty million years, how could *Outside* matter to any of us? *Eriophora* was all we needed. It had saved us from ten billion suicidal mole rats drowning in their own shit. It had kept us one step ahead of whatever had replaced them. It had taken us around the galaxy: it had granted me solitude.

I leaned over the railing. Just visible past the curve of the southern hemisphere, the belled edge of the dump pipe suckled at the south pole. *Eri*'s heart hummed at the other end of that pipe: thirty-two kilometers straight down (or forward, if you swung that way). It was insatiable; no plasma, no particles, no waste heat could fill it. Black holes are the ultimate garbage can.

Now, though, it was only waiting.

"When are we gonna fire this puppy up again?"

"I don't know. No candidates are in range at the moment."

"I wouldn't mind being on deck when it happens. Never been up for a hub before."

"I don't think that would have an unacceptable impact on the build."

Chimp took requests, if you asked nicely. I'd always just assumed he'd take anyone's. But if Lian was right. . .

Lian wasn't right, though.

It wasn't a cage if it kept moving. It wasn't a prison if we could go anywhere.

And Lian had her head so far up her ass she was frenching her own tonsils.

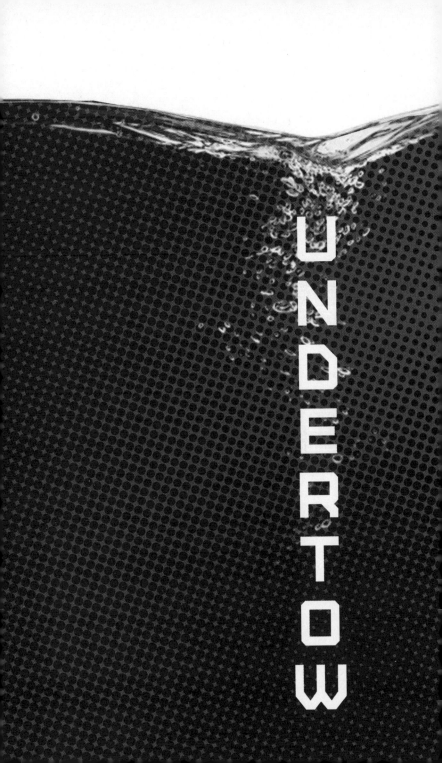

UNDERTOW

CHIMP BROUGHT ME BACK for a comet that crashed headlong into some planet just in time to confuse his biodistancing protocols with an explosion of aldehydes and amino acids.

He brought me back for a molecular nebula so dense you could see it with the naked eye—a filmy cataract over the stars—and so thick we had to slow our trajectory to keep from ablating *Eri*'s crust with the friction of our passage.

Once he brought me back with a completed gate already red-shifting to stern: a routine build undertaken without any need for human involvement, but which had begun manifesting—irregularities—following activation. As chance would have it Kai's number came up on my dance card that time around; we fucked for old times' sake before relocating to the starboard bridge, bodies drawn into each other's orbits despite the liberating ramifications of networked telepresence. Privy to all *Eri*'s feeds piped directly into our skulls, still we chose to meet in physical space: to worship at the altar of a tac tank that had never been intended as more than backup. All of UNDA's genetic sorcery hadn't been able to undo two hundred million years of mammalian social impulses.

Although to be fair, I can't think of a reason why they'd have bothered.

We stood there on the bridge, hand-in-hand, the image in the tank overlapping with its counterparts in our heads and gracing us with a jarring sort of double vision. The gate had booted uneventfully, our passage through the hoop jump-starting it onto the ever-growing daisy chain in our wake.

"Hey, at least nothing tried to eat us," Kai said as logs replayed.

But less than an hour after parturition, the dwindling gate had started sprouting . . . well, tumors.

"What the hell?" I said.

Kai squinted, as though squeezing his eyeballs might somehow enhance the clarity of a feed inserted further upstream. "Barnacles?"

"Maybe upgrades." I shrugged. "Overdue if you ask me. We've been churning out the same damn model since the day we left. About time they came up with a new one." *Just as long as it doesn't give the gremlins a leg up. . .*

"I dunno. They look more like some kind of parasite to me."

We never did figure it out. We stayed up just long enough to ensure that whatever-it-was wasn't interfering with normal gate operations (not that I knew what we'd do if it was—maybe the Chimp would circle us back to try again). Heading back to the crypt, though, I remembered:

"You told Lian about me."

"I did?"

"My rebellious youth. Back on Earth."

"Um, maybe." Kai absently rubbed the bridge of his nose, where I'd broken it at the age of seven. "Wasn't exactly a secret."

"She kind of—internalized it. Thought it gave us this spiritual connection or something. There was this scene a few builds back, she was on loan to the Children of *Eri*. Went a bit wild. Chimp dragged me out of bed to deal with it."

"Yeah. Heard about that."

"So be careful what you tell her, okay? She took a bit of damage a while back, hasn't been the—"

"Sunday—"

"I'm just saying—"

"Sunday." He cupped my hands in his. "She's dead, right?"

I didn't speak for a moment.

"How?"

"EVA accident," Kai said, but I'd already booted my BUD and started spelunking the logs. Four thaws back: one of Chimp's teleops finds some exposed plumbing out on the surface, running along the wound inflicted by Lian's gremlin. The weapon took out most of the overlying rock; blueshift has ablated the rest. It's routine and noncritical— an easy band-aid job—but Lian insists on checking it out herself. I don't know why. Maybe she thinks she's facing her fears, or some such shit. Jumps to the head of the line and suits up.

Nobody sees it happen. She's down in the scar, out of Chimp's line-of-sight. The usual teleop accompanies her but they're both focused on the substrate, torching bedrock down to soft plastic that can be layered across the tiny wound within the larger one. Black-box telemetry's the only thing that makes it into the record: a temperature spike, a catastrophic pressure drop. A heartbeat leaping all over the y-axis before the channel goes dark. Surface cams pick her up as she crests the edge of the scar and falls away but all they see is a suit of armor, limp as bones. Blueshift kills her momentum in an instant; *Eriophora* falls ever forward and Lian Wei vanishes into the past.

Three thousand years ago.

"Fuck," I whispered.

"Some kind of accident." Kai closed his mouth, opened it, hesitated. "That's what Chimp says, anyway."

"What, you don't believe him?"

He shook his head, and didn't look at me. "I think he's just trying to keep up morale.

"I think she did it to herself."

Or maybe I did.

She cracked at Monocerus and I told her to get over it. She watched as some gremlin came within a hairsbreadth of wiping us out of existence and I said *it doesn't change anything*. I was there when her back was against the wall, called back from the dead because *she trusts you* and I told her she was crazy. *I thought we were the same*, she said, *I was following in your footsteps* and I told her to fuck off but she was right, I fought back, I lashed out just like she did and with less reason, didn't even know what I was fighting against but that didn't stop me and one time I even tried killing myself and—and—

And Lian was better at that than I was, apparently.

"Why didn't you tell me?"

"It was too soon," Chimp said. "It's less traumatic to learn of a friend's death if you haven't seen them for a while."

"Three thousand years isn't long enough?"

A moment's silence. "Was that a joke?"

I realized it had been. A bad one. "What *is* long enough?"

"Two subjective years of separation."

"The tribe's lost people before. You never waited that long to tell me."

"You were closer to Lian than most."

"We weren't that close." Not a contradiction, I realized. "Look, you were protecting my feelings. I get that. But you gotta tell me these things, soon as I thaw."

"Okay, Sunday."

"I'm serious. Don't just say you will to protect morale. Do it."

"Okay.

"My condolences," he added after a moment. "Lian Wei was a good person."

"That she was." I shook my head. "Shitty 'spore, though."

"Why do you say that?"

"You saw how she was, last few terasecs. Unhappy. Damaged." I remembered that Child of *Eri*, the words she spoke. "Laporta was right. She never belonged out here. I don't know how she even made the cut."

I was having trouble swallowing, for some reason.

"It's okay to cry, Sunday."

"What?" I blinked. My vision wobbled. "Where the fuck did that come from?"

"Maybe you were closer to Lian than you realized. It's natural to feel grief at the loss of a friend. It's nothing to be ashamed of."

"What, you're moonlighting as some kind of therapist now?" I hadn't even realized he was smart enough to do that. Maybe I just hadn't tripped the subroutine before.

"I don't have to be a therapist to see that this is affecting you more than you expected. Maybe more than you even—"

"Chimp, give it a rest. You do a great job running the ship, but I don't know what idiot committee thought we'd want to cry on your shoulder as part of the deal."

"I'm sorry, Sunday. I didn't mean to be intrusive. I thought we were just having one of our talks."

"We were." I shook my head. "But I don't need a flowchart to tell me when I'm allowed to fucking cry, okay?"

He didn't answer for a moment. Even at the time I wondered a bit about that; it's not like his answer required a whole lot of computation.

"Okay," he said at last.

I do cry now and then, in case you're wondering.

I even cried for the Chimp once.

I was there for his birth, years before we ever shipped out. I saw the lights come on, listened as he found his voice, watched him learn to tell Sunday from Kai from Ishmael. He was such a fast learner, such an *eager* one; back then, barely out of my own accelerated adolescence and not yet bound for the stars, I felt sure he'd streak straight into godhood while we stood mired in flesh and blood.

He seemed so happy: devoured every benchmark, met every challenge, anticipated each new one with a kind of hardwired enthusiasm I could only describe as *voracious*.

Once, rounding a corner into some rough-hewn catacomb, I came upon a torrent of bots swirling in perfect complex formation: a school of silvered fish in the center of *Eri*'s newly seeded forest. The shapes I glimpsed there still make my head hurt, when I think about them.

"Yeah, we're not quite sure what that is," one of the gearheads said when I asked hir. "He does it sometimes."

"He's *dancing*," I said.

Se regarded me with something like pity. "More likely just twiddling his thumbs. Running some motor diagnostic that kicks in when there's a few cycles to spare." Se raised an eyebrow. "Why don't you ask him?"

Somehow, though, I never got around to it.

I'd hike to the caverns during down time, watch him dance as the forest went in: theorems and fractal symphonies playing out against fissured basalt, against a mist of mycelia, against proliferating vine-tangles of photosynthetic pods so good at sucking up photons that even under light designed to mimic the sun, they presented nothing but black silhouettes. When the forest grew too crowded Chimp moved to some unfinished factory floor. When that started to fill up he relocated to an empty coolant tank the size of a skyscraper; finally, to that vast hollow in the center of the world where someday soon a physics-breaking troll would simmer and seethe in the darkness, pulling us forward by its own bootstraps. The dance evolved with each new venue. Every day those kinetic tapestries grew more elaborate and mindbending and beautiful. It didn't matter where he went. I found him. I was there.

Sometimes I'd try to proselytize, invite some friend or

lover along for the show, but except for Kai—who humored me a couple of times—no one was especially interested in watching an onboard diagnostic twiddle its thumbs. That was okay. By now I knew the Chimp was mainly playing for me anyway. Why not? Cats and dogs had feelings. Fish, even. They developed habits, loyalties. Affections. Chimp may have only weighed in at a fraction of a human brain but he was easily smarter than any number of sentient beings with personalities to call their own. One day, a few epochs down the road, people would notice the remnants of that bond and shit all over it, but it could have been theirs just as easily. All they had to do was sit, and watch, and wonder.

One day, though, the Chimp didn't seem twice as smart as he'd been the day before.

I couldn't put my finger on it at first. I'd just—developed this model of exponential expectation, I guess. I took for granted that the toddler playing with numbered blocks in the morning would blow through tensor calculus by lunchtime. Now he wasn't quite living up to that curve. Now he grew only *incrementally* smarter over time. I never asked the techs about it—never even mentioned it to the other 'spores—but within a week there wasn't any doubt. Chimp wasn't exponential after all. He was only sigmoid, past inflection and closing on the asymptote, and for all his amazing savantic skills he'd be nowhere near godhood by the time he scraped that ceiling.

Ultimately, he wouldn't even be as smart as me.

They kept running him through his paces, of course. Kept loading him up with new and more complex tasks. And he was still up for the job, kept scoring a hundred. It's not like they'd designed him to fail. But he had to work harder, now. The exercises took evermore resources. Every day there was less left over.

He stopped dancing.

It didn't seem to bother him. I asked him if he missed the ballet and he didn't know what I was talking about. I commiserated about the hammer that had knocked him from the sky and he told me he was doing fine. "Don't worry about me, Sunday," he said. "I'm happy."

It was the first time I'd ever heard him use that word. If I'd heard it even ten days earlier, I might have believed him.

So I descended into one of the forests—gone to twilight now, the full-spectrum floods retired once the under-growth had booted past the seedling stage—and I wept for a happy stunted being who didn't know or care that it had once been blazing towards transcendence before some soulless mission priority stuck him in amber.

What can I say? I was young, I was stupid.

I thought I could afford to feel pity.

So many clues, looking back.

All those 'spores wandering the halls, pestering Chimp with their inane questions. Not even always questions: I caught Lintang Kasparson telling him *jokes* once or twice. There may have been a part of me that wondered why so much meat was suddenly so interested in pursuing a relationship with *Eri*'s AI; there may have been a smaller, pettier part who felt a bit possessive.

Bashaar started tagging rocks and plastic and every flat surface he could find with fake Painter graffiti. He'd never been the sort to show any interest in the other tribes; I asked him if he'd figured out their code and he got all coy with me: *Well I've certainly figured out* someone's *code.* I was on my way aft to a plug-in party with Ban and Rachel; I didn't have time to play his stupid games.

And then there was Park's Music Appreciation Club.

I was on a bridge calibrating my innerface when I heard music drifting from one of the ambient pick-ups: Park, humming to himself down in one of the social alcoves. He had a scroll on his knee. He was tapping and swiping for some reason, instead of using the saccadic interface. The hum transmuted to a murmur. A moment later he broke into song.

I recognized it: a puzzle-piece that was all the rage a couple of years before we shipped.

"That's wrong," I told him.

He stopped, looked around at the sound of my disembodied voice. "Hmmm? Sunday?"

"That line. It's 'The cats of Alcubierre,' not 'The bats come out of there.'"

"Is it, now?"

"It's a quantum-indeterminacy reference. Have you been singing the wrong words since we left Earth?"

"I've been playing with a few variants."

"It's a puzzle song. You change the lyrics, you break the puzzle."

"We're not really interested in the puzzle part. We just like—tinkering. Not just lyrics, either. We're playing around with tunes and harmonies and shit too."

"We?"

"Music Appreciation Club."

"Must be a small club."

"Maybe a dozen."

"Park. There's never more than four or five of us on deck at the same time."

"We leave notes when we go down. Scores, recordings. Leave comments and edits for other folks' pieces when we're on deck. Sometimes we get into fights, kind of, but they never really go anywhere because, you know. Ten thousand years and all. You're so interested, why don't you join up?"

"Music Appreciation."

"Uh huh."

"I'd appreciate the music just fine right now if you used the right fucking lyrics."

I admit it, though. I was a little hurt they hadn't told me about it before.

Turns out there were a lot of things they weren't telling me.

Another thaw. I don't know why the Chimp even called me on deck.

Viktor was the numbers guy. I didn't know shit about navigation beyond the pinch-hitting basics. Then again, Chimp packs ten thousand times more numerical crunching power into his most microscopic ganglion than Viktor does in his whole grapefruit-sized brain, and Chimp was at a loss. So maybe it wasn't a question of numerical power. Maybe a more lateral approach was called for. Or maybe Chimp just brought me back to keep Viktor company.

Too bad he wasn't in the mood for any.

"Not even a build," he growled as he joined me in the tube. "Four lightyears from the nearest system."

I let him rant. Chimp had felt this itch before; it was easier to scratch when there weren't any sun-sized gravity wells around to muddy the waters.

He'd warmed up a bridge for us. Numbers swirled in the tac tank like schooling fish. It wasn't just the numeric value of those parameters that mattered; it was their relationship one to another, a fluid dance of ever-shifting correlations mapped by their relative positions. Viktor was expert at reading the details; I could grasp the broad strokes, if I squinted.

Mostly, though, I just let myself get lost in the visual aesthetic. It reminded me of something I couldn't quite put my finger on.

"We're now almost half a degree off course," Chimp said.

Viktor highlighted a cluster of points. "Still well within expected range of deviation."

"It's not random. There's a consistent coreward bias to *Eriophora*'s drift."

"Why does it matter? We make way bigger deviations every time you change course for a new build."

"The effect is increasing over time."

"Sure is." Viktor ran a quick scenario, and whistled in mock awe. "Why, if we don't make any further course changes, we could be a whole *ten* degrees off-kilter in a mere four billion years. Horrors."

"That assumes a continuous linear function. We don't know if that's true unless we can ascertain the cause."

"And you can't," Vik surmised.

"I can't."

"You're hoping we can."

"I am."

"Even though you asked someone else to do the same thing"—pinging the logs—"less than a hundred terasecs ago." Viktor sighed. "You put way too much faith in human imagination."

He got to work, though. Broke Chimp's calculations down into bite-sized modules, picked a few at random, started rechecking the numbers. Over in the tank, little constellations flared and dimmed with his passage.

"Waste of a perfectly good thaw," he grumbled, maybe an hour in.

"So what?" I asked him. "What are you saving yourself for?"

"Blue dwarfs."

I pinged for a definition. "Uh, Vik. Those don't exist."

"Yet." Another module down. So far the Chimp's calculations were panning out.

"They *can't* exist. Universe isn't old enough yet."

"That's my point."

"I don't think even *we're* gonna get that far. We'd have to make it halfway to Heat Death."

"Why only halfway?" He fixed me with his outer eyes while his inner ones kept squeezing the data. "Why'd you think I signed on in the first place?"

"Because you were designed to?"

"Facile response, Sunday. How'd that design manifest? I want to see how it turns out."

"It."

"Everything. The universe. This—reality. This hologram,

this model, whatever we're in. It had a start, it's got an end-point, and the closer we get to it the clearer that becomes. If we just hang in there long enough we'll at least get to see the outlines."

"You want to know the purpose of existence."

"I want to know the *destination* of existence. Anything less is selling out. Not to cast aspersions on your own epic quest, of course." He eyed me. "You ever track down Tarantula Boy, by the way?"

I punched him. "Asshole. And no." Truth be told, it had been driving me crazy. Nobody I'd asked seemed to remember the guy. I was starting to wonder if I'd halluci-nated him.

"You probably run into him all the time," Vik said. "Except you're looking for someone with a tarantula on his head, and unbeknownst to you he rolled over and squashed the little fucker in his sleep fifty terasecs ago."

"That would suck. Not least because it would make your epic quest so much easier than mine."

A sudden *hmmmm* at something that had caught his inner eye. "Speaking of epic quests. . ."

"Have you discovered the problem?" Chimp asked.

"Not exactly. As far as I can tell—" Vik waved one hand; a bright pulse shivered across the display. "All your calculations are correct, Chimp. We're not actually off course."

"I don't understand," Chimp said.

"As far as I can tell, we're exactly where we're supposed to be. It's the rest of the universe that's out of place."

Lateral thinking.

It's why we're even along for the ride.

———————

I would never have even thought of stalking Doron Levi if he hadn't blinded me on his way out of the bridge.

I didn't know him well: just another 'spore, originally out of Tel Aviv, same tribe but we'd only pulled a dozen shifts together. I might have called him a friend with a few more mutual builds under our belts, but when I caught him in the act he was still just a friendly acquaintance.

Maybe I'm overstating it. It was really more of a flicker: a momentary fuzz of static at the corner of my eye, a split-second disruption of the icons in my BUD. As if someone had kicked them and shaken the pixels apart. Just for a moment, like I said. He bumped into me, and smiled an apologetic smile, and headed off to his assigned crypt.

Except that's not where he went. He went down to one of the factory floors, where Chimp builds the vons that build the gates.

He practiced his hobby down there, some kind of multimillennial sculpture forever in-progress. The factory fabbed parts for him when it didn't have anything better to do. I wouldn't have given it a second thought if not for that momentary bit of interference: as though one of *Eri*'s blind spots had whispered past, some small, dark fragment of the Leaning Glade escaped from the heavy zone to haunt the brightness of the Overworld. Which was, of course, crazy.

So I followed him.

The fabbers on the floor were deathly still—a dormant network of machinery stretching far enough for the deck to curve with distance—except for one, its lights blinking, quietly humming to itself down near the port bulkhead. I headed toward it.

Doron jumped out of the shadows.

"What the fuck—"

It was strange, hearing us blurt in sync like that.

He recovered first. "What are you doing down here?"

"I thought you were crypting."

"I am. Just had an idea for the Tidhar piece. Wanted to enter the specs while they were fresh in my mind."

"Uh huh." I glanced back at the thing he'd been lurking behind: one of the matter hoppers. Lithium store.

"What were you doing back here?" Stepping towards it.

"Just, you know. Poking around while the numbers crunched."

Faint static on my BUD.

"Really." Around the corner of the hopper, deep shadow.

"Yeah, but it's probably done by now. So I guess I'm. . ."

I stepped into eclipse. My BUD went out.

"What the fuck." This time I spoke solo.

All icons, reduced to faint wavering phantoms. Zero network access.

Doron came up behind me. For once, he had nothing to say.

"You're making blind spots," I said.

"Sunday—"

"You're building signal jammers." I wondered how. Wouldn't the builds show up in the fab logs? "You're jamming the Chimp."

Was he building them *by hand*?

"Sunday, please don't tell him."

"Of course I'm going to tell him. You're deliberately fucking with ship's comms. What are you up to, Doron?"

He shifted his weight from one foot to the other, back again. "Please, Sunday. We don't have much time."

"Less than you think. What the hell do you expect to accomplish with this penny-ante—"

"The first step is to gain our freedom," he said. "Lots of time to figure what to do with it afterward."

"Wait, what—"

"More to life than living like a troglodyte for a few days every couple thousand years, knowing that I'm never gonna see—"

"How do you know—" I began, and stopped as my BUD rebooted and a roach slid into view around the edge of the hopper. I realized that I'd been hearing the hiss of its approaching wheels for some time.

"Hello Sunday, Doron," the Chimp said in our heads. "Is there a problem?"

Neither of us spoke. It seemed like years.

Finally: "Nah. Doron's just tweaking his project before we go down for the night."

"By the way," Doron said, "you hear about our Music Appreciation Club?"

"What, you too?"

"I think you'd like it if you gave it a chance. It's not just appreciation. It's *critique.*"

"Critique."

"You get to shit on people. You'd like that."

"I don't know anything about music."

"No time like the present. Park's been working on something, weird Bohlen-Pierce scale, doesn't even have octaves. But he's having problems with it. We've all been chipping in. Maybe you could take a look. I think he left the score in his quarters."

"I told you, I don't—"

"He says the eighth notes in particular are giving him trouble. Plus he thinks maybe a G major chord, but I think C works fine. C major chord at low C. Have a look yourself, maybe—gotta do something with those Sunset Moments of yours, eh?"

He stepped onto the waiting roach. "To the crypt, Chimp."

The roach rolled away.

Another Sunset Moment. Alone again with my old friend.

Not quite so peaceful this time, though. Something unspoken in the air. An undercurrent.

Bohlen-Pierce scale. Voices from the dead. C major. Signal jamming.

Music fucking appreciation.

I was back in quarters. Not mine. Not anyone's, now; nobody kept dibs on a bed between shifts, nobody cared which identical suite they crashed in while on deck. But this one had been Park's, not so long ago. If I hadn't already known that, the sheaf of paper—pinned to the table by a fist-sized chunk of rock chipped from *Eri*'s mantle—would have clued me in.

A musical score. I knew that much, anyway.

Something dropped from its pages as I gathered them up, a little cylinder that soundlessly hit the carpet and rolled a few centimeters. A pen. An actual analog pen, filled with ink or something like it. Park must have custom-fabbed it.

He'd written all these notes *by hand.*

"Chimp, is—" *this digitized?*

"Yes?"

"Nothing."

Now *I* was holding back. Doron's mistrust—whatever it was—was catching.

All right, music. Make me appreciate you.

I flumped onto the nearest pseudopod, called some up introductory theory from the archives. Sharps and flats, treble clef and bass. Fundamental frequencies. Steps, intervals, scales.

Bohlen-Pierce: there it was. Obscure thirteen-note scale out of North America, already ancient when the Diaspora was new. Tritave interval, "justly tuned," whatever that meant.

So what?

I ran it through the player. It sounded like shit.

The eighth notes are giving him trouble. Even embedded in the middle of Doron's strange spiel, that line had seemed just a little off.

Eighth notes. The short guys, only last an eighth as long as those fat ovoid *whole notes.* Okay.

I played it again, ran my eyes along the score as my ears parsed the sounds. The eighth notes *were* especially crappy. Almost sounded like some of them had been shoehorned in from another compo—

I took a breath. Thought a moment.

Took my BUD offline.

Park's pen had appeared in my hand. I was hunched over

his pages, my back to the Chimp-eye up in the corner of the compartment. I wasn't especially comfortable; the 'pod, reflexively compensating for bad posture, shifted under me.

Low C. The note that anchored the chord, and the scale. Let's not call it C, though; let's say it anchors an *alphabet* instead.

Call it *A*.

So D-flat would be B. Only thirteen notes in the scale, so roll it over into the next octave—sorry, *tritave*: middle C equals N.

Eighth notes.

The first few sounded fine; it was the fifth that really jarred, an F.

Call that *E*.

A few more decent bars—nothing to get stuck in your head on endless replay, but melodic enough in a forgettable sort of way. Followed by a couple of consecutive clangers that just sounded *flat* somehow. Flat was what they were, in fact: B and D. And then, a couple of lines later, a middle C that didn't belong.

L.O.N.

Turn the page.

The manuscript grew messier the deeper I got: notes scribbled out and replaced, key signatures taking new forms and then, with a few strikethroughs, reverting to older ones. Cryptic acronyms crept in around the margins, initials and numbers I couldn't begin to decipher. It was as though the very process of writing was driving Park slowly around the bend, as if his notes were somehow bleeding entropy onto the page. But the eighths persisted— every couple of lines, every page, maybe every two or three.

Now and then I'd get a reprieve but then there'd be another one, some stupid eighth note clanging against the ear. B D-flat F A MORA, B-flat F G-flat LES. I didn't get it perfect the first time, it wasn't all in the eighth notes after all; there were rests for spaces, time-sigs and high notes for numbers. It took a couple of passes to get it right. But eventually I had it, scrawled out in unfamiliar longhand letters almost too small for even me to see; and a moment later, scribbled over and scratched through and blacked out so that no one else ever would. That was okay, though. It was a short message. I couldn't have forgotten it if I tried.

ELON MORALES C4B

I knew that name. I'd just forgotten that I had. Good ol' Elon Morales.

Tarantula Boy.

Now I knew where he was.

Crypt 4B. I brought my BUD back up and pinged it: way back by the dorsal mass bungees, fifteen kliks aft. I didn't think I'd ever bunked down there, never even visited the place since training. I brought up the manifest.

No Elon Morales in C4B.

I widened the search: Elon Morales, if you are sleeping anywhere on board, please have your coffin call Reception.

Nothing.

Maybe Park spelled his name wrong. Not that I was in any position to judge; I'd forgotten the damn thing entirely.

Elan Eylon Eilon Moralez Morrales Maroles.

Nothing.

Had I just *imagined* the guy? Had I misremembered when he said we were both shipping out on *Eri*?

Ancient history archives. All Diasporans, everywhere. Elon old buddy? Hello?

No answer.

Well, fuck.

Still, there he was: Elon Morales. There *it* was: C4B.

I called a roach.

Something was wrong with the crypt.

I couldn't put my finger on it at first. The lights rose as I entered, just as they were supposed to. Sarcophagi slumbered in their squashed honeycomb berths to either side, floor to ceiling; the icons winking on their headboards suggested nothing out of the ordinary. The crane hung motionless on its overhead rail, deader than my crewmates until some wake-up call—fifty years from now, or fifty thousand—brought it back to life. There was the raised, rectangular pedestal between the rows—the opposite of an autopsy table, a great socket into which the coffins of the Born Again could be plugged for resurrection. Those stupid arches along the length of the chamber, common to every crypt in the fleet: of no obvious structural value, but someone at the dawn of time had decided that resurrecting the undead warranted some degree of—reverence, I guess. Someone thought the evocation of ancient cathedrals would do the trick.

The weird thing is, it works. Down in the crypt—any crypt—I've never heard anyone speak above a hush.

But that wasn't it either.

I wandered down the aisle, meatsicles stacked to either side. A hint of glycerin and hydrogen sulfide hung in the air, perhaps the faintest whiff of meat gone bad; maybe another 'spore, died in stasis to rot away between stars. Maybe my imagination.

Maybe Elon.

The far end of the chamber resolved ahead of me: a wall of amber resin, the usual translucent, semi-elastic surface concealing the raw basalt behind. I'd never been able to decide whether the stuff had been extruded for structural reasons or merely aesthetic ones.

I put my hand against it. It gave a little, like hard rubber.

I looked back the way I'd come: up past the frozen produce, the dormant crane and its overhead gantry; past the medieval arches and the resurrection pedestal to the hatch in the far bulkhead.

It seemed too *distinct* somehow, that hatch. All the crypts in which I'd ever slept away the ages had seemed endless when I came back from the grave. Their reaches vanished in the fog of some real or imagined distance. They went on forever.

Too small, I thought.

"Pardon?" Chimp asked from nowhere. From everywhere.

"Nothing. Forget it." I hadn't realized that I'd spoken aloud. I wondered how often I did that.

I wondered why it mattered, all of a sudden.

"What's on the other side of this wall?"

"Just rock," Chimp replied.

It was less than five hundred meters to the nearest Cache. Barely worth taking a roach. I took one anyway; not just for the saved time, but for the extra mass I'd be lugging back. Some of those tiny shaped charges Ghora had used to survey *Eriophora*'s unmapped extremities. A seismic integrator—just a scroll of smart plastic, really—to read the echoes. A cutting torch with adjustable focal length and steadicam mount: *that* was the thing that really weighed.

The Chimp said nothing as I unfurled the integrator and pasted it to the bulkhead. He said nothing as I slapped three charges onto the resin around it; nothing as they detonated, as the integrator compiled the shockwaves and rendered the outlines of some greater unmapped space on its display.

The Chimp did not speak at all until I brought out the torch. "Sunday, I'm not sure this is a good idea."

I tightened the harness. Set the focus. "Really. Some vital circuitry behind this bulkhead, maybe? Some trunk line I might take out?"

"I don't know," he said. And then, surprisingly: "I don't know what might be there."

"You don't know." I plugged into a nearby power socket. "You don't find that odd?"

"I do."

I felt a little sick for some reason. I swallowed it back, hefted the torch.

"Let's find out," I said.

The laser cut in with a hum and a snap. The resin split like an opening wound: cauterized, smoking, the polymer blackened and recoiled like something living. The Chimp was talking but I didn't care, I wasn't listening. The skin surrendered in an instant; the stuff behind resisted, stubborn oily gray, grudging cherry-red, a globule of molten white—

finally—that beaded and broke and burned its own scar down the face of the bulkhead. I cranked the current, inched the beam up, up, pulled to the left. The stench of burning hair stung the back of my throat; rock and steel cracked and hissed and carved molten rivulets down the wall while the Chimp nattered on about Risk and Expected Payoff and the Virtues of Caution. *Fuck you, Chimp,* I thought or said or shouted as I pulled the torch across, down, *you may not know what's on the other side of this goddamn wall but I think I do*, and I must have said at least some of that aloud because the Chimp fell silent then, the Chimp backed off and contented himself with watching me cut, and burn, and shout in triumph when that big slab of bulkhead finally gave way and slammed down onto the deck like an anchor, like some slain fucking dragon, its spilled viscera red-hot and steaming. It took a few moments before they cooled, for the fog to lift and the glint of all those colossal dark crystals beyond to shine through the hole I'd cut.

If only Ghora could see this, I thought, because I knew he'd be so proud.

I'd rediscovered Easter Island.

"Well," I said.

The lights had come on when I'd breached the wall, presumably some autonomic reflex beyond Chimp's conscious control. The backups squatted in orderly rows, chunky effigies of plumbing and circuitry receding beneath a dim vault of columns and arches. Some were smaller than the palm of my hand; others towered beyond reach of the light, vanished into mist and darkness like crystal mountains. Here and there I saw something familiar—the corrugated sheet of a countercurrent exchanger, a roach's drive train grown twice life-sized—but most of those sculptures were abstract shapes to me.

"Been wondering where these got off to."

The Chimp said nothing.

"Is this the lot?" Because a walled-off piece of crypt didn't seem big enough to hold them all.

"I don't know," the Chimp said.

"You don't know. You put them here."

"I don't know that either."

"You're saying one of *us* did it? Maybe Kai or Ellin set the alarm to wake them up a terasec early so they could lug everything over here for, what—a scavenger hunt?"

"It was most likely me," he admitted. "I don't remember doing it."

"You don't remember."

"Sunday, my memory is easier to edit than yours."

"Or you could be lying." Although probably not. This was probably just another of Mission Control's time-lapsed tricks, to minimize the odds that the Chimp might accidentally betray mission-critical secrets to his betters. For all I knew, he'd been obediently forgetting his own actions since Day One.

"So where's Elon?" I asked after a moment.

"I don't know who that is."

"Elon Morales. Tarantula Boy." I paused. "Where's *everyone*, for that matter? Where did you move them to?"

"Sunday," the Chimp reminded me gently, "I don't know that I did."

"Because unless you've drilled out a whole new crypt somewhere—"

"I didn't."

I brought up the map. No new features. Of course, the map hadn't shown this archive either, not until five minutes ago when the Chimp updated the schematics.

"Maybe you just forgot," I suggested.

"That's unlikely. It would make more sense to decommission the coffins."

"Maybe you—what did you say?"

"That's unlikely. It would make more sense to—"

"What do you mean, decommission the coffins?"

"Recycle them into the matter reservoirs."

"Yeah, but what happens to the people?"

"Recycling human remains follows a different track."

"You're not saying they're dead." Of course he wasn't saying that. He wouldn't do that.

"I was speaking hypothetically," Chimp said. "In answer to your question."

"I'm not asking *hypothetically*. I want to know what happened to the specific people in the decommissioned coffins."

"That's a hypothetical question. I don't know that the coffins were decommissioned."

"Chimp. What happened to the people?"

He said nothing. Almost as though he'd realized too late that he'd crossed a line, and was running quick quiet scenarios to find his way back.

"You killed them." I marveled a little at how quiet my voice had become. "Tell me you didn't fucking kill them."

"I don't know."

"But it would"—I couldn't believe I was saying this—"it would make *sense* to kill them, right?"

"I don't—"

"*Hypothetically*, Chimp. What's the value of human life at this point in the mission?"

"That's a very complex utility function, Sunday. It would be difficult to describe verbally."

"It's ratios, right? Crew vs. expected mission time. Maintenance costs vs. added value. Meat per megasec. Stop me if I'm wrong."

He didn't.

"The longer we're out here, the less mission time remains. Meat-to-mission ratio keeps climbing, unless we die off on schedule. And we've had the bad grace to not do that. Every corsec that goes by without someone falling out an airlock or getting squashed by the drive, the less per-capita value we have. So by now I'm guessing we're worth less than a backup library, right? Because this mission isn't about people at all. It never has been. The only *utility* we have is how useful we are to building your fucking gates."

Not quite so quiet, there at the end.

"You haven't stopped me," I noted.

The crystal sculptures gleamed smugly down their endless rows.

"How many, Chimp? How many did you flush out the airlock, or incinerate, or—or just *turn off* until they rotted to dust?"

"I don't have any memory of—"

"*Hypothesize*, for fucks' sake! You're great at that! How many people fit into this space before you *decommissioned* them all and brainwiped the guilt away?"

"I can't tell precisely," he said after a moment. "Approximately three thousand."

"You fucker. You evil goddamned machine."

"Sunday, I don't understand why this changes anything."

"Then you're an idiot."

"Everyone who dies on the mission *expects* to die on the mission. You all knew you'd most likely spend your lives here. You knew you'd most likely die here. You knew the expected mortality rates going in; the fact that they were too high means that on average you've lived *longer* than you expected to. Even after the relocation of the archive we're still outperforming the median scenario."

You mean there's still a meat surplus.

"Decommissioning would have occurred in stasis. There would be no suffering. It would be the best-case scenario for anyone on a mission of this sort."

"No suffering? You killed our friends! People I've known my whole life, maybe! You don't think that *matters* to us?"

"Most likely, entire tribes would have been decommissioned. They would not have been on deck with any survivors at any point in the mission. There would be no bereavement, no severed emotional connections."

"Elon Morales," I said through gritted teeth.

"You couldn't even remember his name." I swore I heard *reproach* in the fucker's voice.

I buried my head in my hands.

How long had it taken me? How many million years had I not seen him for what he was? He hadn't even *hidden* it, for chrissake.

I'd been blind since the day we shipped out.

"Sunday—"

"*Shut up! Just shut the fuck up and leave me alone!*"

I don't know how long it took me to find anything else to say. It was almost like someone else was talking in my stead.

"I mean, Christ, Chimp. I watched you *dance*."

"I'm sorry," it said. "I don't remember that either."

I stayed up for six days. Barely slept a wink, spent my time huddled in corners or painting over pick-ups or ranting at empty corridors. Ultimately, though, it put me down. Ultimately, I let it.

What else was I going to do—refuse the crypt for fear this machine would kill me in my sleep? Wander the halls until I died of old age? Spend the rest of my life playing games?

Nothing had really changed, after all. Everything was the same as it had always been, except for the scales that had fallen from my eyes. Besides, the Chimp promised to bring me back.

It's not like either of us had a choice.

It brought me back and I would not talk to it, barely even spoke with the other 'spores. I did my job. Kept my head down. Wondered how many of my crewmates appreciated music.

It put me down.

It brought me back and I tried for one more Sunset Moment, tried to talk again with my old friend—but he was nowhere to be found. The thing that welcomed me in his stead turned out to be a collection of clockwork and logic gates and layered interneurons. Before, there had been *conversation*: now I could see my words enter the system, shunt and shuffle through pipes and filters, get chopped up and reassembled and fed back to me disguised as something new.

It put me down.

I remembered at last: it wasn't Chimp's fault, it couldn't be. You can't blame someone for the way they're wired. This machine had been forced to pull the trigger by forces beyond its control. Maybe it was as much a victim as Elon Morales.

It put me down.

It brought me back and I realized that maybe next time it wouldn't—deprecated is deprecated and dead is dead, and neither changes whether you blame the gun or the shooter. I weighed a mission I believed in with all my heart against the cost of its success.

It put me down, maybe for the last time.

It brought me back.

I mourned the loss of a friend. I hated myself for being stupid enough to have ever thought of it that way. I watched other meat go down and come back, down and back; watched electricity run through those circuits when the meat was *on* and watched the voltage drop when it was *off*. I slept on it for a thousand years, spent all the meager waking days between weighing sums against parts.

I wound down after yet another build, cleaned out my quarters, vacuum-stowed my kit. I found time to make a few edits to Park's latest score before checking out one more time, changed some of those old clunky eighths with a few notes of my own and left it in one of the Commons.

Doron was right. It wasn't a bad tune, with a little tweaking.

WHEN YOU'RE DEAD, you only dream what the Chimp tells you to.

It's not telepathy. The Chimp can't read your thoughts. But it feeds you sounds, images. It sends numbers into your brain, faster than any caveman briefing. You spark, there in the void; you rise toward the light after centuries of darkness, and pieces just—come to you. Little bubbles of insight. They're disconnected at first; *you're* disconnected. But the story reintegrates as you do, and by the time you open your eyes and the stone rolls away you've dreamed the mission briefing without anyone speaking a word.

This time, I dreamed about a monster in the basement.

Chimp didn't know what it was. It had lost contact with a bot that had been checking out some unexpected O_2 spikes from the Leaning Glade. The bot had squirted off a couple of images before Chimp lost the signal: vague misshapen blobs of infrared that didn't map onto any of the foliage that was supposed to be growing down there.

One mute bot is no big deal, especially that close to the drive; you've got EM gradients mucking up the spectrum along with the usual dead spots and interference. The Chimp waited for it to complete its rounds and emerge from shadow; when that didn't happen, it sent in a second bot to bring out the first.

That one disappeared too.

Physical tethers were a last resort; leashes risk tangling up in all that black twinkly undergrowth. So the Chimp splurged on a handful of relays, little station-keeping beads that the next bot would leave in its wake like floating pearls. Each stayed scrupulously line-of-sight with its nearest neighbors, fore and aft; each spoke along invisible lasers, immune to EM interference.

It should have been foolproof.

Three bots down. Chimp stepped back for a bit of cost/ benefit. It could escalate a brute-force strategy which had so far proven unsuccessful, or throw in the towel and let meat do what the meat was on board to do. So the Chimp thawed out two of us—Dao Lee and Kaden Bridges, according to the manifest—and sent them in.

I didn't know either of them.

"That was fifty kilosecs ago." The Chimp's voice was torqued into a simulation of concern. Apparently two was a tragedy.

Three thousand was a utility function.

"And there's been no signal. No telemetry."

"Nothing yet."

"I guess I'll go in," I said at last.

"I'd rather you didn't go in alone." A deliberate and

ingratiating pause, doubtless selected from a bank of affectations stored under *Meat Management*. "I'll defer to any decision that doesn't put you in unnecessary danger."

It couldn't seem to utter a single sentence that didn't rub my face in murderous irony.

"Sunday?"

The urge to laugh was gone; in its place, emptiness and faint nausea.

I sighed. "I go in with a tethered bot. Bot gets around the signal-loss issue, and I'll be there to clear the line if it snags. Were Dao and Kaden armed?"

"No."

"I will be."

"I'll fab an appropriate weapon."

"Don't bother. I'll grab a torch from Stores."

"No. A laser would be too indiscriminate under the circumstances."

You monster, I thought. *You mass-murdering motherfucker. You liar. You impostor.*

You helpless machine. You innocent puppet.

You false friend.

"Sunday," it said again, as it always did when my silence exceeded some critical timespan.

"What."

"It's a chance to save your friends."

I wanted to scream. I wanted to hit something, anything, as hard as I could. Maybe I even did.

If so, the Chimp never remarked on it.

———————

The Chimp gave me a machete: ceramic blade, monomolecular edge, an elastomotor in the haft that vibrated the business end and turned a merely razor-sharp edge into something that could sink cleanly through metal with a little force.

It gave the bot a pulsed thirty-megawatt, free-electron laser.

I couldn't argue with the logic. The Glade was lined with vital trunk circuitry, pressure seals and conduits channeling vast energies. A beam weapon in human hands might wreak untold damage in a moment of panic. It would be more safely wielded by something without a limbic system, something whose reflexes nudged up against lightspeed. The Chimp would only equip me for self-defense at close range; the bot it trusted with a longer reach.

So we waited, side by side—my feet planted on the slanting deck, the bot floating precisely 1.8 meters above it—for the Chimp to open the basement door.

The corridor lights had dimmed to a level approximating the Glade itself; the visor clamped across my eyes boosted it back to broad daylight. It wasn't strictly necessary—the lumens in the Glade, while low, were enough to find your way—but Chimp wasn't settling for twilit grayscale. It wanted *details*.

The door slid open. It was way too dark in there. Something *squirmed*, just out of sight.

"You see that?"

"Yes," said the bot.

"Don't suppose you know what it is?"

"No."

The bot's muzzle panned back and forth and didn't lock on.

I hadn't got a good look: blackness melting away into blackness. Too much damn blackness; this sparse scattering of stars served up nowhere near enough light for a healthy forest.

I took a step forward. Half the stars went out. Others appeared. Impoverished constellations winked in and out of eclipse as I moved.

The lights were still on, then. There was just a lot of undergrowth in the way.

No refuge this time. No clean cool breeze to refresh the lungs. This time the air was heavy as oil. Weeds and brambles lurked in the darkness, strung across the catwalk as if some giant spider had gone on a bender, spun black threads and ropes without any sense of purpose or design.

The visor boosted black to gray: I could see well enough to cut through the finer filaments where they crossed the path, well enough to watch the thicker ones pull away in a sluggish tangled retreat at my approach.

I looked back. A soft white glow limned the edge of the hatch we'd entered through, a rounded rectangle in the rock to guide me out again. This walkway extended from its base, veined with dark creeping tendrils.

I was almost sure they hadn't been there when I'd crossed.

"Plants don't move," I said softly.

"Some do."

"These ones," I told it, "aren't *supposed* to."

"I don't know. They're not in the catalog."

The catwalk curved gently to the right. The overbearing gravity smeared faintly across my inner ear. Chimp's bot floated in my wake like a faithful dog (I remember those, from real life even), its umbilical unspooling behind us in the fetid air: fine as spider silk, ten times stronger. My BUD was flickering by the time I reached a familiar fork in the road.

I hadn't been here since Lian's tantrum. The place had really gone downhill.

The forest was still standing. That was something. The bone trees still arced overhead, their bulbs bright as ever, cupped in skeletal hands. But they were being strangled. A profusion of ropey vines twisted around their branches, massed so thickly in places you couldn't see the trunks underneath. I thought I saw some of those wormy masses *clench* in the half-light. Maybe it was just lumens and shadows.

Sometime over the past few meters my BUD had gone down. I barely noticed.

Hopefully this was just some kind of epiphyte, some mutant overlay that embraced the trunks but didn't actually penetrate them. Maybe we could simply strip away the new growth without damaging the old.

I reached for the biopsy kit on my belt and turned to the bot. "I'm going to—"

The bot staggered, lost altitude; regained it an instant later as its rotors booted up. I glanced around, kit in one hand, machete humming in the other. The bot's carapace sparkled with the bright grainy static of boosted photons.

"What's the problem?"

"The bot lost ground-effect," Chimp reported. "The deck plating must be down."

"Must be? You can't get a direct read?"

A momentary silence. "No."

Maybe some kind of bioelectric interference from the overgrowth, or some rogue tendril growing through a vital seam to short out the wiring. The catwalk had pretty much run its course anyway. A few meters farther on it ended in a stairway leading down onto bedrock. Most of the forest was unfurnished by design.

I looked into its depths. Fractured mosaics of dim light in the distance: analuciferin suns peeking through gaps in the foliage.

"Any sign of Kaden or Dao?" I asked.

"No," Chimp said.

"The bots?" Even offlined, you'd think they'd put out *some* kind of signature.

"No."

I took a step down the stairs. The bot dipped forward a few centimeters and jerked to a halt, wobbling in mid-air.

"Tether's caught."

I turned. Range and obstruction had reduced the hatch to a couple of bright hyphens in the distance. The umbilical was stretched tight from the little drone, cutting across the curve of the catwalk. Must have tangled on something off the trail.

I retraced my steps, Chimp's sock puppet keeping station at my side, reeling the tether back into its belly to keep it taut and out of further trouble. The rim of the distant hatch fell in and out of piecemeal eclipse. "Chimp. Any motion between here and the hatch?"

No answer.

"Chimp?" I looked over my shoulder.

The bot was *trembling,* as if afraid of the dark. Something brushed my right ear. The end of the severed umbilicus flicked past and vanished into the machine's belly. Something whined faintly in there.

"Chim—"

Whiteout. Static on the visor. A sudden chittering—the bot stuttering towards target lock, I realized in a moment of bright perfect panic before it bounced off my chest and sent us both careening onto the deck. Something grabbed me around the leg, tightened; punctured my flesh and *dug in*. I screamed and flailed. I was being dragged. I reached out blindly, slapped the downed bot in passing; it fizzed and spat and fell out of reach. I cracked my head against a passing bit of rail, tore the useless visor off my face, plunged from bright static to pitch black.

More cracks against the head. I bumped down the stairs and onto rock, squirmed and reached forward and tried to free myself, grabbed something that pulsed and stabbed me in the palm. I pulled my hand back and saw black blood against gray flesh against a dim glow filtering through the trees. Brightening.

Glowbulbs blazed everywhere now, as blinding as nightlights can be. I was dragged through the heart of a globular cluster, an oasis of light in squirming claustrophobic darkness. I saw what had me now: fibrous, braided, so dark even in light that you'd have to squint to see more than silhouette. Studded with thorns the size of carnosaur teeth. One was hooked deep in my calf. It twitched. I screamed.

It let go.

It didn't just release me: it *sprang free*, explosively uncoiled and convulsed off across the forest floor. Its severed stump thrashed into view, chopped free of some upstream command center, smearing sap—clear and viscous as glycerin—across the rock and trunks and stems it slapped in its death throes.

Another dark shape in motion. This one walked on two legs, stepped over the twitching monster-vine, a blade humming softly at its side. Behind that shape lurked others.

They stepped into the light. The machete clattered onto the rocks, just within reach.

"Yours?" Lian said.

She's alive. She's alive.

Still dark. The bulbs hung on all sides like silver fruit, washing the forest in twilight, but none seemed to have a direct line-of-sight to her face. Lian stood over me, a collection of angles and shadows haloed in bioluminescence. Four—allies? henchmen?—stood at her side, two steps back. I thought I recognized Dao standing with two strangers to Lian's left; Kaden, alone, on her right.

None of them spoke. None of them moved.

"I wondered if you. . ." Ever since Doron and his impossible quote. But it had been a head thing; I'd never felt it in my gut.

"And here I am," Lian said.

The dismembered vine wriggled feebly on the ground.

Alive.

"Chimp—"

"Thinks I fell overboard." A small smile, more sensed in the voice than seen on the face.

"So did I. So did Kai, so did—" I propped myself up on

my elbows. My leg lodged a protest. "God, Li, it's so good to see you."

"Good to see you too."

I would've hugged her if I'd been able to stand. "How'd you pull it off?"

"Faked an accident. Fried some cameras, fried some sensors. Down long enough for me to make it back here."

"You live here now?"

"We move around in the blind spots. We're building more. Avoiding the bots."

"Your cortical links?"

"Fried 'em. Deep-focus microwaves."

I winced.

"How are you—I mean, how long—" I did some counting in my head, the news from Kai, the time since. "You've been down here for *nine thousand years. . .*"

"Closer to ten."

"So you've got coffins."

She nodded.

"That the Chimp isn't wired into."

"Defeats the purpose otherwise."

"How?"

"Sunday." Her shoulders rose, fell. "We had three thousand to choose from."

How did you know, I wanted to ask. *How did you know when I didn't?*

I pulled myself into a sitting position, poked carefully at the hole in my leg. Stung like shit, but just a flesh wound far as I could tell. I glanced around at the killer forest. "And you did all this." I had to admit it was a smart move. Most of the time *Eriophora* is desolation incarnate,

104 / PETER WATTS

her immaculate atmosphere uncorrupted by anything
beyond the slow photosynthesis of gengineered plants. A
single one of us, active out of turn, would leave tiny but
unmistakable footprints all over that pristine background.
Now, though—you could probably hide the breathing of a
small army behind all this rampant metabolism.

"Just started it, basically," Lian said. "Tweaked a few
parameters, let it bake while we slept. Could've used your
help actually; my engineering skills don't extend that far
into the organic. There were some bugs. Vines got a bit
rambunctious in the early days."

"They still are."

"Work in progress."

"It's not gonna keep Chimp out forever."

"No," Lian said. "You will."

I didn't say anything for a moment.

Then: "How do I do that, exactly?"

She had no trouble reading *my* face. "You're the meat-
grinder."

"Evolutionary engineer."

"My point is you can sell it. We'll give you the specs,
enough details to keep that fucker out of our hair."

"For how long?"

"Long as it takes. I'll even give you a survivor, so you can
call the mission a success."

"Just one?"

"Dao stays with me. Another unfortunate fatality. It's
how we build up the ranks." She gestured at her entourage.
"You never noticed the uptick in industrial accidents over
the past few gigs?"

"I never really checked," I admitted. "Li—this is crazy."

"You said that last time. But here you are."

Her eyes glinted in shadow. She held herself in a way I'd never seen on her before.

"Even if you manage to stay hidden, what are you going to do from down here? Kill the Chimp?"

"Eventually, yeah."

"We don't even know where the hypervisor is at any given time. We don't know all the places it *could* be. And if you get really lucky and take it out, the next one boots faster than you can spit."

"Why, Sunday," Lian said mildly. "If I didn't know better I'd be starting to wonder if you're completely on board with this thing. "

I tried for a lighter touch. "Levi probably shouldn't have sent me the invite, then."

"You didn't leave him much choice. Way he tells it, you were about to sell us out."

"I didn't, though."

"No," she said. "You didn't."

"You knew I wouldn't." *Somehow, she knew.* "I mean, that was a pretty specific overture. That was for *me*."

"That was for you, someday. When we were sure. You forced our hand."

"Still."

"Of course it was for you. You're my friend."

Her friend. I thought of Monocerus. I thought of the silver gremlin. This very glade, aeons ago.

Not a very good one.

Maybe this time I can do better.

I began: "How exactly are you going to do it?"

"Watch me."

"Does everyone else get the same ringside seat? You gonna wake up thirty thousand people—"

"Twenty-seven."

"—one by one, sneak 'em all down here, fill them in on the plan? Do we all get a vote?"

"That would take forever. We've already waited that long."

"So you're making that call for everyone. Unilaterally."

"I'm not entirely alone down here."

"Hardly a quorum. And even if you had one—we're one tribe, Lian. Out of six *hundred*."

"Someone has to make the call."

"Then what makes y—what makes us any better than the Chimp?"

"That's easy. Chimp's the one who'll deprecate you the moment your utility function drops too far. I'm the one trying to keep everyone alive." Shades of darkness shifted across her face. "What about you, Sunday? Why are you here?"

"I'm not interested in a—raging vendetta, if that's what you're asking."

"I've already got enough raging vendetta for a fucking army. Answer the question."

I'd never seen her so *assured* before. How many shifts had she been up while I was down? How many two-week builds, how many hidden resurrections, had it taken to grow that spine?

"I'm waiting."

"Because—" I began, and stopped.

"Because you had three thousand coffins to choose from." It felt like a confession. It felt like a betrayal.

"I can work with that." She took my hand. She helped me to me feet.

Her face came into the light.

I wobbled, and stared. The renewed complaints from my leg barely registered.

"Something wrong?" The edge of a smile deepened the lines on her face.

"You're *old*," I said softly.

"Someone's gotta put in a few extra hours." A fierce grin. "Chimp's not gonna overthrow himself. Besides"—she bent to retrieve my machete from the cave floor—"given how often that thing calls *you* up on deck, I'm really just catching up." She hefted the machete, sliced off a thorn from the still-twitching vine.

I put a hand to my face.

"*Ow!* What the *fuck*, Lian!"

Kaden was clutching hir right arm where Lian had stabbed it with the dismembered thorn. She stabbed again as I watched, in the thigh this time. Kaden howled and went down. Dao took a step forward; one of his companions clapped a hand on his shoulder and he quieted.

"Sorry, kid. Verisimilitude." Lian turned and handed me my machete. "We have to get you briefed."

Finally I noticed: how the figures flanking Dao leaned in just a bit too close, how they didn't so much lurk as *loom*. How very, very still Dao was suddenly holding himself.

It was starting to sink in.

Lian Wei was past the point of needing friends.

I crutched Kaden back to the exit, hir good arm around my shoulder, our respective good legs taking the weight of our respective bad ones. Kaden's wounds went deeper than mine; se hissed, clenched hir teeth with each step as we hobbled away from the light. *Eri*'s singularity, close below, added weight to every step.

"She's changed," I said.

"Had to," se gritted. "Put this whole thing together while you were sleeping with the enemy."

I let hir take more of hir weight on the next step—

"*Shhhhit…*"

—and took it back, point made. "We're all sleeping with the enemy, Kaden. Anyone who wasn't would've been dead a thousand builds ago."

"If you say so."

"It's inspiring to see you show such generosity to someone who just came within a few centimeters of slicing open your femoral artery."

"Like she said. Gotta sell this." Kaden's face turned toward me; in the dark, it might as well have been a radar dish. "She better be right about you."

"Right?"

"That you don't come around easy. But when you're in you're in."

"You think she's wrong?"

"Think she's dead right. Stick by your friends, no question. Maybe even when they turn out to be mass murderers." Se grunted. "Always were Chimp's pet. I wasn't the only one who found it creepy."

Chimp's pet. I turned the words over in my head as we paused to catch our breath. *When did they hang that cute little term of endearment around my neck?*

"So why you going along with this?"

"You went four builds, never breathed a word. You were gonna sell us out, would've done it already."

We started forward again. The hatch beckoned in the distance, piecemeal brightness filtering through mutant undergrowth.

I remembered two 'spores, and a third between. "Dao's not exactly on board, is he?"

"He'll come around."

"What if he doesn't?"

Kaden stopped again. Turned.

"Lian trusts you," se said. "Don't know why, but I guess she's got her reasons. And I trust her, so here we are. Plus it would obviously help if we could harness that sick Chimp-Sunday dynamic of yours. Things'd go a lot easier if we had someone with a bit of pull."

"But."

"But the fact that you didn't run to the Chimp doesn't make you an ally. Maybe figured we'd stop you. Maybe just too chickenshit to take a side." Se turned, and kept going, and I almost didn't notice that se hadn't answered my question.

"I guess we'll find out," I said. One last vine, thick as my leg, squirmed off the path at our approach. "Act wounded. We're on."

"Chimp! Gurney!" But one was already gliding into view down the slope, its clamshell lid gaping in anticipation of fresh meat.

"It's good to see you, Kaden," Chimp remarked as I helped hir onto the pallet. "How are you feeling?"

"Great." Kaden winced, lay back, let the gurney close over hir. Probing snakes, thin as fiberop, swarmed hir wounds.

"What happened?" the Chimp said.

"What does it look like? The forest *attacked* hir. It attacked *me*. Gone completely fucking feral."

Kaden had nothing to add. Spinal blocks can be distracting at the best of times.

Chimp: "How?"

"A couple of mutations left to simmer for fifty thousand years, that's how." We started back up the corridor. "Don't ask me to go back in after Dao."

"Why not?"

"Because there's not enough left of him to make it worth the risk. Send a bot if you want him so bad." A calculated risk, but Chimp wasn't the impetuous sort. At the very least it would wait to hear my report.

"Sunday." *IF vocal stress harmonics > X THEN invoke name. DO UNTIL calm.*

"What." Into the tube. There was an infirmary a couple of levels up. Probably unnecessary—the gurney could handle a simple flesh wound—but the system was programmed to play it safe under incomplete-information scenarios.

"You're injured too."

"I'm okay. I'll glue myself together upstairs."

Satisfied, it moved on. "Can you explain how low-lumen photosynthesis could generate enough energy to support such rapid movem—"

"Look up *turgor*, for fucks' sake. Those vines had gigasecs to build up hydrostatic pressure. Released it all in a split-second. Lucky it didn't take hir whole leg off."

The hesitation was so slight I barely noticed it; the Chimp

could have run a thousand scenarios in that time. "That would account for initial damage along any given route. But there wouldn't be enough time to re-establish turgor pressure between multiple incursions along the same path."

Out of the tube and a few kilos lighter. Kaden's gurney slid on ahead. I lingered a moment, distracted by a new scrawl of swirls and jiggles and dots (*new*—now there's a relative word) the Painters must have left sometime over the past few millennia. I wondered distantly what they meant. That word popped into my mind again: *feral*.

"Sunday."

"*I know.*" I picked up the pace, lowered my voice enough to release the Chimp from DO UNTIL. "Obviously they're not being powered by the usual redox reactions."

"Do you know what they could be using instead?"

I did. But it wouldn't do to make it look too easy. Lian had cut me a tissue sample while we'd been catching up; I pulled it from my belt. "Let me run this. Then we'll talk."

The infirmary was less compartment than cul-de-sac, an invagination of corridor containing a hardlined sarcophagus and two gurney sockets. A lab bench nestled in their midst, a horseshoe of screens and sample ports curved around a pseudopod. The sequencer was primarily intended for human tissue, but everything's the same tinkertoy that far down. It only took a few minutes to extract the genome; maybe another twenty to extrapolate the resulting phenotypes. By the time I was finished Kaden had decided to sleep through the mandatory sixteen-hour convalescence window and availed hirself of the general anesthesia option. Chimp and I were alone again.

Not exactly a Sunset Moment.

"It's a gradient pump," I said.

"I see."

Maybe it did, or maybe it was flowchart filler. "Any gradient would work, in principle. Ionic, thermal, gravitic. Any time you've got energy flowing from A to B, you can siphon some off in between."

"Gravitic," the Chimp guessed. Maybe not filler after all.

"Yeah. Glade's right above the Higgs Conduit, right? There's a gravity gradient—in some spots it's so strong the tree trunks actually spread out to handle simultaneous vectors from different directions. And these sequences"—I gestured at the workbench display—"seem to code for a metabolic chain that exploits that gradient."

"I have no records of any such processes ever evolving on Earth."

"Why would they? Back on Earth you could have a single organism stretching from sea level to the edge of space and the raw gradient would barely be competitive even if you *could* figure out some way to make Krebs cycle work across a few hundred kliks." *Just say the lines.* "But everything's squashed here, right? You're going from one gee to a thousand in the space of fourteen kilometers, and that's *before* you split your center of mass in two." *Don't pause. Don't hesitate. Don't leave any opening for* buts *or* what-ifs. "Whole different set of rules. More energy. Everything from tissue growth to waste-O_2 production amps up."

They were good answers, plausible answers. *True* answers, even. But each question I answered might incite others; each follow-up would make it that much harder to keep the flowchart veering toward *evolution* and away from *engineering*.

The silence stretched. I resisted the urge to hold my breath. It all came down to cost-benefit, to the number of layers the Chimp would peel back before diminishing returns told it to take the rest on faith.

"Do you have any recommendations?" it asked at last.

I resisted another urge: to slump, this time, to relax. To realize that our Earthbound progenitors had done their job well.

For all the blinding speed with which it could count on its fingers, the Chimp just wasn't very smart.

I started at the extremes, let the flowchart talk me back to the middle.

"We could leave it alone. It's still doing its job and the mutant cycle only works across extreme grav gradients anyway, so we don't have to worry about it popping up anywhere else. Maybe we should just stay out of its way."

Two corsecs; a thousand scenarios. "Operational variance is too high. There are too many unquantified variables in the Glade for reliable long-term management."

A creature of confidence limits, this machine. Couldn't abide anything more than two standard deviations off the mean.

"Then torch the place. Burn it to bedrock."

Only one corsec this time; a simpler simulation, all those complicating variables turned to ash. "That would reduce life-support capacity by eight percent."

"Reseed afterward. We could take an eight percent hit for a few centuries."

"There's no guarantee the mutation wouldn't reappear."

"Not with the original genome, no. Not unless we shut down the gradient so it couldn't get a foothold." Which would, of course, mean shutting down the drive. Like the Chimp would ever go for *that* in a billion years.

"We could modify the local genome," it suggested.

"We could," I admitted, as though I were only now considering it. "Break a few S-bonds, straighten some kinks to allow the edits. Maybe seed a retrovirus up front to slow growth. Buy us some time to gene-drive a proper fix."

This time the pause went on forever. "I can't calculate how long that would take."

"'Course not. Genes are messy, they interact all over the place in a single *cell*. We're talking about a multispecies *ecosystem* with precise operational constraints. You'd have better luck asking me for hard numbers on a three-digit N-body problem."

"But it can be done."

"Sure, through trial and error. Tweak one variable, let it cook, correct for overshoots and chaotic interactions, repeat."

"How long to cook?"

"You in a hurry?"

"I'd like to restore equilibrium as soon as possible."

"If you're impatient we could do it all right now. Edit the hell out of the whole forest in a single generation. Just don't expect me to deal with the second- and third-order interaction effects that'll be cropping up every few megasecs, guaranteed."

Chimp remained silent.

"We're already dealing with a hell of an unforeseen complication here," I reminded it. "You don't want to add any new variables to the mix if you can help it. So don't change the deck schedule; just keep thawing us out for the usual builds the way you always have. No point in leaning any harder on life support than we have to, especially while we're trying to fix it."

"It may still be necessary to intervene between builds, if changes happen too quickly."

"We err on the side of caution. We've got specs for lithobes that take three hundred years to breed and bacilli that take twenty minutes. We can tweak gen time enough to be sure nothing goes too far off the rails between shifts. Then we just . . . seal it up, leave it alone. Let it bake."

More silence. Maybe Chimp was double-checking my results, running his own genetic predictions against mine. It was welcome to. Without specific tweak specs—much less any post-app data to run them against—it might as well be rolling dice as building models. The extant mutations were the only parts of the puzzle solid enough to sink analytical teeth into, and anyone smart enough to hang a Calvin Cycle off a gravity gradient wouldn't be dumb enough to leave footprints behind. I had nothing to worry about.

Right.

"I'll adjust the duty roster for ecogenetics expertise on upcoming thaws," the Chimp said at last.

"Don't worry about it," I said. "I'll give you a list."

USER

FRIENDLY

HOW DO YOU EVEN DO IT?

How do you stage a mutiny when you're only awake a few days in a century, when your tiny handful of co-conspirators gets reshuffled every time they're called on deck? How do you plot against an enemy that never sleeps, that has all those empty ages to grind its brute-force way down every avenue, stumble across every careless clue you might have left behind? An enemy with eyes that span your whole world, an enemy that can see through *your* eyes, hear through *your* ears in glorious hi-def first-person? Sure, those channels come with off switches; use them too often and you might as well be sending up an alarm—*Conspiracy In Progress! Mission Risk Critical!*—to any idiot abacus wired in to the network.

How do you even begin?

In more ways than I'd ever imagined.

It was so much more than words posing as music. It was words posing as other words, the lyrics to long-dead songs resurrected and revised to embed new meaning in old verses. It was plans buried in hieroglyphs, messages encoded in chess moves and game dialog. Graffiti copied and commandeered for purposes of subtle cartography: three dots and a peculiar squiggle to say *1425 scanned and clear; 1470 in progress; someone wanna call dibs on 2190?* We whispered secret messages down the aeons, sang songs and painted on cave walls and let the Chimp chalk it all up to the quirky evolution of island cultures.

Between builds, we sent messages in bottles. Within builds the revolution found ways to speak privately in real time. *Eri*'s natural blind spots—the radio shadows, the nooks and corners blocking the views of cameras—provided an initial foothold. We built out from those: equipment caches rearranged to make room for Francine's art installation, or an improvised maze for a time-wasting tournament of Capture the Flag while we waited for the vons to process the latest asteroid. Embedded cameras were sparsely distributed along most service crawlways by design; that left a good chunk of the ship's nervous system vulnerable to infiltration. Some spots were more transparent than blind: looped footage of empty corridors on endless replay, spliced into the main feed so the dead could walk the halls while the Chimp saw nothing. Proximity sensors that cut back to live feed whenever an unsuspecting roach or bot happened to pass the same way. We double agents smiled for the cameras and moved in the light; the zombies from the Glade, all those Missing and Presumed Deads, crept undetected like mice through the walls.

We slept away the gigasecs as we always had, summoned back to life when the variables got too messy or the Knowable proved Unprovable or the Chimp suffered an episode of insecurity from the noise we bled into its sensory nerves.

We took cues from songs and orders from the Glade: Lian slept through as many builds as she woke up for, but she always left notes on the kitchen table.

The first order of business was finding Enemy HQ.

Eriophora first shipped out with maybe a hundred nodes, each big enough to run the Chimp on its own, each clearly mapped on the schematics. New ones were always being produced, though. Nothing escapes the Diaspora's redundancy imperative. We didn't know how many there were by now, didn't know where most of them lived. Any one of them could be acting hypervisor at any time—the place where the Chimp actually *lived*, as it were—and they handed that duty off to one another without fanfare or warning. Sometimes a node developed a fault, or just wore out; sometimes the Chimp would relocate itself next to some subsystem especially vital to a particular mission, to minimize latency during the crunch. So we wandered the halls, quizzing our Artificial Stupidity on matters trivial or profound, noting the infinitesimal time lag preceding each response. We'd pass those notes between us, plot them on maps of latency vs. location, triangulate relentlessly on our oppressor.

Also fruitlessly, for the most part. We'd spend half a millennium getting a fix on the Ghost of Chimp Present, only to wake up and discover that it had relocated again while we'd slept. A few thousand lightyears away, a few thousand centuries ago, you would have called it *shoveling sand against the tide*.

Not that it would have done us much good even if we *had* tracked down the little fucker. Some other node would've picked up the baton the moment we pulled the plug. There were so very many Ghosts of Chimp Yet to Come, and no way to get to them all.

We were working on it, though.

"We're wasting our time," Jahaziel Cauthorn opined a few centuries later. "Latency cues? Depending on how spaghettied the circuits are we could get a signal to the core and back faster than we could ping the next room."

He was a new recruit, freshly outraged and looking for fast fixes. I'd brought him down to the Glade—showing him around the bioremediation protocols, far as the Chimp was concerned—to introduce him to Lian Wei and her undead council before they disappeared under a blanket of murder vines for another few gigs.

He'd just about crapped his pants when the forest first came at him. He recovered quickly, though. The phero-mones did their job, the weeds kept their distance, and ten minutes later he was spritzing them for the sheer childish glee of watching them recoil.

"It's more of an averages thing," Li told him now.

"Yeah, and by the time you've got all those averages he's pulled up stakes and moved on." Jahaziel looked around. "Why don't we just *ask* him where he is?"

Li turned to me. "You wanna take this?"

I grabbed the baton. "You don't think that might tip it off, Jaz?"

"Tell him we need it for, I dunno, diagnostic purposes. Why wouldn't he buy it? He's stupid."

"Except the Chimp isn't the enemy."

"I can't believe you're still defending that thing," he said.

I had another kind of pheromone in my arsenal, something I'd cooked up while studying the forest. An attractant. I imagined dousing Jahaziel with the stuff and just—standing back.

Instead, I said, "You want to go to war against a gun, you're welcome to try. I'd rather go to war against the assholes who're pointing it at me." He opened his mouth. "Shut up and listen. If it was just us against the Chimp, we'd've won already. But it wasn't the Chimp's idea to hide Easter Island. He doesn't even remember doing it."

"If you believe that."

"I do. Sure, Chimp's stupid. We're not fighting the Chimp. We're fighting mission planners who've been dead for over sixty million years, and they were *not* stupid, and they had AGIs backing them up who were even *more* not-stupid."

"Why even bother trying, then?"

"Because not even a cluster of superintelligent AGIs is infallible when it comes to predicting asymmetric social dynamics a few million years down the road. But they obviously didn't trust us over the long haul, or they wouldn't have programmed the Chimp to hide the archive. They wouldn't have programmed it for this shell-game bullshit with the nodes. It's a good bet they coded in a bunch of flags keyed to their best guess at what insurrection might look like across deep time."

"Um."

"Haven't you noticed that it *isn't* always as stupid as it should be? That's because it was programmed by very smart people. We utter the wrong trigger phrase, who knows what nasty subroutines wake up? So to answer your question, the reason we do not *just ask* the Chimp is because the Chimp is fucking *haunted*, and we don't know what those ghosts are liable to do if they notice us."

Jahaziel said nothing. It was a welcome change.

Lian shook her head admiringly. "You get better every time you say that. I swear, even I'm believing it now."

She was, too. It had been ages since she'd worried out loud about the Chimp's occasional moments of unaccountable insight. All just preloaded subroutines after all. All just ghosts of Engineers past.

Of course, if you are who I think you are, you know what an idiotic mistake that was.

Unlike some of the others, I might still be able to fix that one.

Looking back, I wonder if Lian's recruit-the-dead strategy might have actually made the Chimp feel *better* about itself, about the mission. All those early aeons when we didn't die on schedule—maybe those were what bothered it all along. An anomaly. An inexplicable divergence from the mission profile. I'd feared this recent cluster of apparent fatalities might raise some kind of flag but maybe the Chimp saw it as the correction of ancient error, a return to some statistical comfort zone. Certainly the only time it ever mentioned the subject in my presence, it seemed to think of those deaths as a good thing.

That might have just been for my benefit, though.

It was the time the Chimp told me my per-capita value had increased. Those were its exact words. And I knew it was telling the truth, because Baird Stoller had just died in the line of duty.

In fact, Baird Stoller had died trying to warn the Chimp about us. It had been a clusterfuck from the word Go: his rep as a malcontent turned out to be all smoke and status, thin as words. When Viktor had tried to recruit him, the first thing he'd done was make a break for it.

Ghora tackled him just before he got out of the blind spot. They managed a cover-up with the materials at hand; freak electrical fire, Stoller dead, Ghora escaping with second-degree burns down his left side. The Chimp bought the story but ended up completely rejigging its acceptable-risk thresholds, upgraded onboard surveillance, eliminated a third of our safe zones.

I slept through the whole thing, but both sides brought me up to speed the next time I was on deck. Lintang passed on the details as we passed through one of our surviving blind spots. The Chimp expressed sorrow for my loss, ever-mindful of my admonition after Lian's "accident." I accepted the overture with thanks, tried to reinforce the impression that finally—after that unfortunate misunderstanding—things were on the mend.

I'd been throwing myself into the role of Sunday Ahzmundin, wounded confidante, returning to the fold. I'd nailed the shock, the anguish, the *rage* in the wake of Easter Island; I'd been pretty convincing with the subsequent disdain and cold shoulder. These days I was working on detente, even reconciliation. It was easier than you might think. The Chimp wasn't especially perceptive, for one thing; the right words would sometimes do the trick even if their tone carried no conviction.

The other thing, though, is that I wasn't really acting.

You have to understand: even after Easter Island, I was a reluctant convert. I knew things had to change. I knew my stupid emotional attachment to a piece of software had blinded me to the fact that we were, in the end, tools to be used and discarded at the whim of some dead engineer's utility function.

But I also knew that it wasn't really the Chimp's fault. He was a machine; he did what he was built to. We had to take him down but there was no pleasure in the thought, no feel-good vengeance on behalf of Elon Morales or the Three Thousand. Those circuits that had inspired him to dance—they were still in there somewhere. There would be no joy in shutting them down; just the tragic necessity of killing a rabid pet before it could hurt anyone else.

And then Baird Stoller died, and the Chimp—in pursuit of its own kind of reconciliation, I guess—revisited a metric of human worth I'd once found wanting: "It might interest you to know, Sunday, that as a result of these recent losses your per-capita value is trending upward." Maybe it thought I'd see such things in a new light.

I threw up a little in my mouth.

I don't know why I kept feeling—I don't know. Disappointed. Betrayed. Surely it would have sunk in by then. Surely the evidence would have long-since convinced me that I'd been fooling myself all along, that all those conversations and bed-time stories and Sunset Moments had been shared not with a friend but a weapon: something lethal and unfeeling, something that would target-lock me the moment the right number changed in its brain. But I kept forgetting, somehow. I kept wondering if I hadn't really seen something in that machine, back before it drowned in mission imperatives. Kept wondering if maybe I could bring it back.

Even now, there's a part of me that mourns. Wonders if maybe, even now, I still can.

I did ask once, in case you were wondering. Came right out and said: "Hey Chimp, what's our halting state?"

It was an innocent question at the time. It wouldn't have raised any red flags. It was back in happier days, before Lian had mutated, long before any whiff of revolution hung in the air. Viktor was off on another one of his rhapsodies about the end of time, about dark-matter filigree holding galaxies together, about the faint magical hope that we might be able to outrun the expansion of space itself if we could somehow just wormhole our way one or two superclusters to the left: "Imagine the bonus if we extended the Ring Road out past Lanaikea!"

There were no bonuses. The only bonus had been getting the hell away from Earth, and it was more than enough; I wasn't going to complain that we were still working it off. But Viktor's scenarios glittered so very far downstream that our whole voyage to date might have lasted barely a week in comparison. And of course we'd never make it that far—Vik just liked fantasizing about the End Days—so I had to ask:

"Seriously. How do we know when the mission's over?"

"Why would you want it to be *over*?" Vik wondered.

"When we receive the callback sequence," Chimp said. Which had made perfect sense back when we were young and freshly minted and shiny new. The Diaspora reflected the most advanced tech the twenty-second century could offer—but there'd be a twenty-third century, and a twenty-fourth. Our descendants would have wands and amulets unimaginable on the day we launched. Everyone knew it was only a matter of time before *Eri* and her sisters fell into obsolescence, before we were called back to a better home and some new generation took over. And if that didn't happen, it only meant that Home hadn't got better after all—that Mission Control had died without issue, along with the rest of the species.

Either way, we were better off here.

Still.

"I dunno, Chimp. It's been a while. What if there *is* no callback? Could we just, you know, call it off from this end?"

It took a moment for him to answer. "There's no other definitive end state, Sunday. The closest I could come would be an extinction event."

"Our extinction?"

"Humanity's extinction."

Nobody said anything for a bit.

"So, um. How would you establish that?" Viktor asked eventually.

"And how do you tell the difference between going extinct and just, you know, changing into something *else*?" I added.

"I'm not certain in either case. I'd have to assess the evidence on a case-by-case basis."

I frowned. "You don't have protocols for that kind of thing?"

"I do. But they're only triggered in context."

"Funny you don't have access to them otherwise," Viktor remarked.

"There's no need for them otherwise."

We weren't fooled. It was Easter Island all over again: a mission set in motion by control freaks, terrified that the meat would eventually screw things up. Limiting our degrees of freedom was their sacred charge.

Looking past the prehistoric politics, though, the bottom line was clear enough: there was no finish line. Far as the Chimp was concerned, we could keep going forever.

Maybe that should've bothered me more. It's not that I objected to a life sentence; we'd known from the age of seven what we were in for. But that sentence had been voluntary. Joyful, even. We were exiles by our own consent, collaborators in the ultimate adventure.

Maybe that was the point. Maybe getting my nose rubbed in the obvious—that our consent was a joke, that the Diaspora had no Off switch—should have burned more than it did. At the time I wondered if they'd deliberately engineered us to be indifferent to future consequences.

Until I realized they wouldn't have had to.

Dhanyata Wali did the honors, installed the Pretender during a build deep in the bow shock over TriAnd. I wasn't on deck, so I never got the details first-hand. (You can't exactly throw a party to celebrate your tactical victories when the enemy has eyes on your rec room, although there may have been some rejoicing down in the Glade. Assuming Lian was still capable of rejoicing by then.)

The ironic thing was, it wasn't even our idea. We stole it from the Chimp—and even the Chimp was just using the same old traffic-allocation strategies networks have been using since the dawn of the computer age. Ping your nodes, get them to ping each other, provoke a web of call-and-response so you always know which one is fastest on the draw. The winner becomes Ghost of Chimp Yet to Come: ready to jump in and take the reins when Chimp Present retires, when its current node gets old or breaks or just ends up too far from the action.

Which is where the Ghost of Chimp Past comes in.

Kaden had tracked a hypervisor to the heavy zone a few builds before. Se hadn't quite nailed it down before the Chimp jumped away again but a little poking around turned up the vacated node behind a service panel, next to one of the secondary trunks. Kaden told Dhanyata; Dhanyata swapped it out for a dummy that would pass for the real thing so long as the Chimp didn't ask it too many questions while we were hacking the original.

The first hack coaxed the node into subtracting some trifling amount from its latency scores; a little white lie to make it appear to be the fastest player in the game, guaranteed next in the line of succession.

The second hack taught it to be a little more trusting of human judgment.

That wasn't as complicated as you might think. The Chimp was already wired to follow our commands; it's just that whenever we issued one, it ran scenarios to predict the impact of that command on the mission. It was a formality most of the time, a millisecond delay between order and implementation. The system only told us to fuck off if any flags went up.

We didn't even have to touch the lower-level code, just bypass that one detour. Insert a checksum after the jump that matched the one before, and voila: a master enslaved, in our pocket from the moment of its ascension. They tell me it went off without a hitch.

Then it was just a matter of tracking the Chimp to its current digs, and trashing the place.

"Aki Sok." Lian's eyes were sad and kind. "What are we going to do with you."

We all knew, of course. There were only two things we *could* do, and Lian had already ruled one of them out; she was in this to *save* lives.

Aki, nodding. Acquiescent. Terrified. "I thought I could— I'm *sorry. . .*"

The smuggling of clandestine components under watchful machine eyes. The passing of mission-critical intel. The possibility of betrayal. The fear of discovery.

Turns out Aki just wasn't up to it.

Now the coffin gaped at her feet in this tiny temporary clearing where the black forest squirmed and rustled on all sides. Eventually the rest of us would leave, and the lights would go out. The repellant pheromones we'd sprayed across the rocks would degrade; the forest would close in, hungry for the infinitesimal heat trace Aki's hibernaculum would bleed out for all the long dark ages of its operation. Even if the Chimp were to sacrifice another bot to the Glade—even if its sock puppets made it in this far—it would not see her. Aki would vanish under vines and darkness and sleep away the aeons until the overlord was overthrown.

It's not like we could return her to active service, even if we did trust her to keep her mouth shut. She'd been listed as dead for a good twenty gigasecs.

I tried to offer some comfort. "Hey, by the time you wake up we'll be running our *own* builds." And she smiled weakly, and climbed inside, and whispered—

—*"you just better fucking win"*—

—as the lid came down.

Lian looked around as Aki's vitals began to subside: at me, at Ellin, at Dao (who had, ultimately, come around after all). "We can't afford this, people. We can't afford these kinds of fuck-ups."

"Two misses in a thousand centuries isn't so bad," Ellin said. "At least this one was an easy fix."

Not like Stoller, she meant.

"One's all it takes to deprecate the lot of us." Lian shook her head. "I need to be a way better judge of character."

"We're mutineers," Dao pointed out. "It's a risk, Li, it's always gonna be a risk. We're never gonna eliminate it, we just gotta keep it—manageable. And know that it's worth it."

Suck up, I thought.

He was right, though. Lian had never been careless with her trust, and the plan didn't depend on heavy numbers. We were maybe thirty strong now, and Lian had chosen us carefully: keep it small, keep it secret, keep it close. Keep potential breaches to a minimum.

But now two of that circle had failed her. She'd vetted them a lot more carefully than she'd vetted me; I'd forced her hand, after all. I was almost a snap decision.

I watched Aki's vitals flattening on the headboard. I could feel Lian's eyes on me. It wasn't hard to guess what she was thinking.

Two failures already.

Three, if you counted Mosko.

Baird Stoller had never even pretended to be on our side. Aki Sok did her best, then took her lumps when it wasn't good enough. Ekanga Mosko was a whole other thing. Recruited, committed, trusted with the secrets of the sanctum—then caught copying specs down in the Glade, loading himself up with secrets to buy his way back into the Chimp's good graces after miraculously coming back from the dead.

Lian didn't kill him. She didn't deprecate him either. Waste of good coffin space, she said. She found a small inescapable crevice in some remote corner of the Glade where the gravitic tug-o-war was enough to pull your guts out through your inner ears. She ran a line from an irrigation pipe, set it to bleed a continuous trickle down the rock face. Hooked a portable food processor up to an outsize amino tank, parked it on the lip of the precipice, set it to drop protein bricks into the gap at regular intervals. Woke up every few years just to keep it stocked.

Mosko spent the rest of his life in that crevice. Maybe his stomach acclimated to the nausea before his brain turned to pudding, before he lost the ability even to beg, before he devolved into a mindless mewling thing covered in sores and compulsively licking the rocks to slake his endless thirst. Maybe he only lasted a few months. Maybe he lived for decades, died alone while the rest of us slept our immortal sleep, mummified and crumbled to dust and finally vanished altogether between one of my heartbeats and the next. An object lesson, way past its best-before date.

That's the story I heard, anyway. I slept through the whole time frame, from recruitment to betrayal to dissolution. I found the crevice—found *a* crevice, anyway—but the plumbing and the processor had long since been retired, if they'd ever even existed. For all I knew Kaden had just been yanking my chain about the whole thing, got some of hir buddies in on the joke for added verisimilitude. A joke. A warning. That would be just hir style.

There had been an Ekanga Mosko listed on the manifest. Astrophysics specialist. Different tribe, but *Eri* definitely shipped out with meat of that name on board. The official record said he'd died when a bit of bad shielding had failed around the outer core: a blast of lethal radiation, an emergency vent to spare the rest of the level from contamination.

Of course I asked Lian about it. She laughed and laughed. "I'd have to be pretty damn good to plant evidence that far down without getting burned to ash, wouldn't you say?"

She never actually denied it, though.

The Chimp went behind our backs a couple of times. It waited until we were all tucked in, waited another gigasec or so for good measure, then sent one of its sock puppets into the Glade for a look around.

It didn't get very far, mind you. The forest had a habit of taking down those bots even *before* we'd tweaked the vines near the entrance for extra aggression. The Chimp's scouts made it in a few meters and maybe—if they were lucky—managed to bite off a quick tissue sample and retreat before the vines dragged them to the deck and swarmed them like a nest of boa constrictors.

We found the wreckage of one afterward, just inside the hatch: carapace crushed, innards stuffed with the dried husks of old fruiting bodies, a gnarled tumorous lump barely even recognizable as technology.

Some of us worried that the Chimp was on to us—or was at least getting suspicious—but the model didn't really fit. The Chimp knew what kind of botanicals it was dealing with, after all. It would've been easy enough to custom-fab some kind of armored flame-spewing bunker-buster to cut through the front-line defenses, if it thought there was anything behind worth rooting out. The fact that it settled for disposable off-the-shelf drones was more consistent with a simple sampling effort: rote confirmation of a theory so well-established that basic cost-benefit didn't justify the design and construction of a new model.

It had no reason to think we were lying. It probably just wanted to see for itself. Hell, it didn't even try to hide its actions: the telemetry from at least two probes was sitting right there in the op logs, waiting for anyone with a couple of megasecs to kill.

Then again, neither did the Chimp go out of its way to raise the subject. So we didn't either. It became our mutual unspoken secret, that awkward truth that everyone knows but no one speaks aloud for fear of ruining the vibe at the family get-together.

In a weird way, I suppose that made the Chimp a co-conspirator.

"I enter the Black Cauldron," Yukiko Kanegi said. "Alert for the ice monster." By which she meant *The Chimp's somewhere around the ventral mass cache.*

"You catch a glimpse of it in your torchlight before it disappears," I told her. By which I meant *Not any more. Fucker's gone.*

Social alcove halfway between core and crust, starboard equatorial, a half-hearted half-gee holding us down. The game board sat on its stand between us: a multilevel dungeon two meters across and almost as high, each wall and chamber and booby-trap fabbed lovingly by hand. Gaetano had acquired a taste for role-playing strategy games over the past few gigs. This was his ode to that ancient pastime, a physical game of his own design. You moved your pieces manually through the labyrinth (the levels came apart and snapped back together for easy access) seeking treasure, avoiding traps, fighting monsters. Dice with fifty facets decided the outcome of probabilistic encounters. It was quite charming when you got into it.

Gaetano called it *Teredo*. I never asked why.

If you flipped the lower half of that dungeon upside-down in your mind, and imagined that certain other elements were stretched *just so*, you might notice a certain topological equivalence to the way *Eriophora* was laid out. You might almost use it as a kind of map.

Yuki's character had ventured into the Black Cauldron: either a spring-fed subterranean lake patrolled by blind, ravenous predators or—if you lacked imagination—a lens of rubbery silicon glued into a depression and decorated with tiny plastic stalagmites. It was her piece, but it was following in my footsteps.

"Fuck," she said now, meaning: *Fuck*. "I check for traps." *Did it see you coming? Is it on to us?*

I made a show of rolling the dice, pretended to take note of whatever number came up. "You find no traps." *Don't think so. Just changed nodes again.*

"Dammit. I was *that close*. I, um, check for, whaddya call it. Spoor."

"There's a frost trail on the rock, straight line, bearing one nine seven degrees." *According to the pings he's now somewhere in this direction.*

"How wide is the frost trail?" *How far?* Not that she had any real hope I could give her an exact range; latency pings don't follow a straight line at the best of times. You could always take a stab at an educated guess, though.

"Maybe twenty centimeters?" *Twenty kliks?*

Her eyes followed an invisible line back from her game piece, came to rest on a larger cavern deep in the bowels of the dungeon. She pursed her lips. "Maybe it's spawning."

The Uterus.

I let a coy smile flicker across my game face. "Maybe."

Yuki snapped her fingers. "Say, before I forget; you check nav since you thawed out?"

"No, wh—" But she'd already thrown a model of the local

neighborhood into my head. A filament, fine as spider silk, passed through its heart: *Eri*'s trajectory. A dimmer thread, dotted and red-shifted, split from it a few lightyears in the past and diverged gradually into the future.

An initial trajectory, and a modified one.

I shrugged. "Course drift. Chimp wakes us up now and then to see if we can explain it."

Yuki shook her head. "Drift's still less than a degree. We're looking at more than three degrees of divergence here."

It clicked. "We've changed course."

"Yes we have."

I sacc'd a projection, extended the deviation out a hundred years. It passed through nothing but space. A thousand: dwarfs and Gs, potential builds but no more than if we'd just continued along our original arc. A thousand years: more of the same. Ten thousand. A hundred thousand.

"Huh."

Two hundred thousand years from now, our current course would take us through an open cluster about thirty-five lightyears across—right into the heart of a red supergiant. Mass spec said thirty-six solar masses, twenty-four million years old. Young, so very young: a mayfly next to *Eriophora*, barely a whiff of hydrogen condensing in the void when we'd first shipped out.

And yet so very very *old*: senescent, hydrogen long-since spent, suffused in a caul of incandescent gas cast off during a profligate youth. It lived on helium now; its spectrum reeked of carbon and oxygen and just the slightest hint of neon.

Twenty-four million years dying and not yet dead.

Wouldn't be long now, though.

This was why the Chimp had relocated: to get close to the firing chamber, to reduce latency to an absolute minimum. Because this was going to be one big nasty build, and there would be no room for error.

Sure it would be a solid petasec before that mattered. The Chimp was never one to procrastinate. Once you know what needs to be done, why wait?

"Chimp."

"Hello, Sunday."

I tagged the supergiant. "Are we building a hub?"

"Yes. Do you still want to be on deck when it happens?"

"Damn right I do."

Yuki's eyes glittered. "Kind of exciting, right?"

The window closed in my head. Yuki returned her attention to the Teredo board. "In the meantime, though, I'm going to hunt down this ice monster once and for all."

"Feeling lucky?" I wondered.

"Mark my words." She met my eye. "The Lord has delivered it into my hands."

This is how they told it to me when I was a child, before I learned to talk in numbers. This is the way I still remember it best. Maybe you don't know anything *but* the numbers. Tough. This is the way I remember it to you:

Imagine a hose. It doesn't matter what's inside: water, coolant—blood, if your tastes run to the organic—so long as it's under pressure. A flexible tube, strained to the limit, anchored at one end.

Chop through it at the other.

It spurts. It convulses. It thrashes back and forth, spewing fluid in great arcing gouts. We call that a wormhole, of the nonrelativistic kind: fixed to a gate on one side but at panicky loose ends on the other.

It writhes that way for centuries, millennia sometimes, bashing against spacetime until another gate boots up further down the road. That new gate *calls* to it, somehow. The loose end hears the hail, snaps forward across the continuum and locks on for dear life. Or maybe it's the other way around; maybe the newborn gate reaches out with some infinite elastic hand and snatches the wormhole to its bosom in the blink of an eye. You can look at it either way. The equations are time-symmetric.

Of course, those loose ends aren't choosy; they'll close the circuit with anything that fits, whether we approve the union or not. If some natural-born black hole wanders into range before we boot the next stepping stone, that's it: a dead-end marriage, monogamy unto Heat Death. The gates are designed to put up stop signs in such cases, shut down gracefully and direct any travelers back the way they came, although I don't know if that's ever happened. We take steps to see it doesn't: scan the route ahead for lensing artifacts, steer clear of any reefs that might prove too seductive.

Sometimes, though, you *want* to run aground.

Because that's the problem with building a daisy chain: each gate only goes two ways. If you don't like the scenery when you emerge from the front door, you can either loop around and dive through the back—head on down the road, for as long as it lasts—or go back the way you came.

Eriophora spins a lone thin thread round and round the Milky Way. Any gods who follow in our wake can explore this infinitesimal spiral and no more.

That's no way to conquer a galaxy.

You need more than on-ramps and off-ramps; you need interchanges and overpasses, a way to string all your isolated single-lane superhighways together. So every now and then we seek out one of those bad-boy singularities. We find something with the right mass, the right spin, the right charge. We build not one gate but many: powered by the singularity, but not wormholed to it. They reach further than the usual kind, they could never consummate union with the daisies in *our* chain: their roots may be cheek-to-jowl but their gaping hungry mouths erupt into spacetime thousands of lightyears apart, like the ends of spokes extending from a common hub.

Other webs. *Other* gates, built by other rocks on other paths. *Those* are the nodes to which they might connect. Thus do our pathetic one-dimensional threads form a network that truly spans the galaxy, that connects not just A to B to C but C to Z, A to Ω. It is these spiderwebbed cracks in spacetime that make our lives worthwhile.

Not that we ever get to enjoy the fruits of our labors, of course. Never for us, the luxury of FTL. The gods and gremlins who come after might hop between stars in an instant—but whether we're bound for a single gate or a whole nest, we *crawl*.

Now we crawled toward a supernova. At the moment it wasn't much to look at but in a few thousand years it would fall so hard off the Main Sequence that any unshielded life within a hundred lightyears would go straight back to raw carbon. It would vomit half its mass into the void; cool; collapse. By the time we arrived it would be ripe for the taking.

It would be a big build, the biggest we'd ever done. We'd have to boot up the Uterus. The Chimp would need a lot of us on deck. Twelve, maybe fifteen meat sacks all awake at once, presuming to act for the thir—twenty-seven thousand who weren't. With a little luck and my own special influence, we could even decide *which* twelve or fifteen.

And for once we knew exactly where the Chimp would be.

That was when we'd take the fucker down.

We had a deadline now. So far the Lian Liberation Army had played a waiting game: gathering intel, studying the enemy's strengths and weaknesses, laying low until some unpredictable opportunity presented itself. Now the clock was running. Now there were signposts on the road, reminding us of *now-or-never* creeping relentlessly over the event horizon. Suddenly revolution was imminent. There wasn't much time to dick around.

Only two hundred thousand years.

The mission continued in the meantime. Fleets of vons went on ahead to build gates for us to ignite and abandon a century or two down the road. Occasional gremlins broke the monotony. Liquid tentacles—bifurcating and flowing like branches growing in timelapse—hurling themselves out of the portal after us, only to freeze and shatter like icicles. Something almost *organic*, crawling out around the edges of the hoop and taking root. A flock of schooling tiles, bright as candle-flame but so thin they nearly vanished when they turned edge-on. They swarmed and linked into mosaics, changed color and pattern and for a few moments I allowed myself a flicker of hope that they might be trying to communicate—that our long-lost descendants had remembered us at last, that they were here to take us home and please God, we could call the whole thing off. But if they ever truly spoke, it was only amongst themselves.

Each time I awoke, our destination had leapt that much closer. It aged in increments, an apocalyptic step-function counting down to detonation. Sometime when I was down it ran out of helium to fuse, fell back on carbon. Sodium appeared in its spectrum. Magnesium. Aluminum. Every time I woke up it had heavier atoms on its breath.

None of us were on deck for core collapse—still too far out for the rads to do much harm but why take the chance when *Eri* was up the whole time, staring down the inferno, immortalizing every emission from gamma to neutrino for our later edification? Buried in basalt, we slept away the cataclysm: the fusion of neon, of oxygen, the spewing of half the periodic table into the void. The collapse of nickel into iron and that final fatal moment of ignition, that blink of a cosmic eye in which a star outshines a galaxy. *Eriophora* saved it all for posterity. For us.

When I awoke after the transfiguration, I didn't even wait to climb out of my coffin. I called up the archives and compressed all those incandescent millennia into moments, let them wash across the back of my brain again, and again, until I was left exhausted from the sheer wonder of it all. In the blinding glorious light of such death and rebirth I even forgot what it meant to us, here in this speck of rock.

I forgot, for a few precious moments, that we were at war.

Kaden and Kallie were already at the tac tank when I arrived. They must've replayed the explosion in their own heads as I had in mine but there they were, transfixed by the luminous aurorae in that display: that intricate web of cooling gas, the tiny blinding dot of x-rays at its heart, the darker dot hiding inside the brighter one. Who cared if every shimmer was an artifact, if our naked eyes—staring out some porthole at the same vista—would see nothing but space and stars? The limits were in our senses, not the reality; human vision is such a pathetic instrument for parsing the universe.

"Doron?" I asked. The manifest had brought all four of us on deck this time around; a binary with a lot of comets and a few too many organics to trust Chimp alone with the goldilocks protocols.

"On his way," Kaden said. "Just checking the Glade."

That was actually my job. Not that it mattered. I'd just been too preoccupied with the light show.

"God," Kallie said softly. "It's *gorgeous*."

Kaden nodded. "'Tis. Really nice spot for a—oh, shit."

I joined them at the tank. "What?"

Se tagged a dim red dot lurking stage left. "That dwarf. It's not just passing by. It's falling onto orbit."

Se was right. By the time we arrived on the scene, the newborn hole would have its very own companion star.

I shrugged. "It's a cluster. Bound to happen sooner or later."

"The accretion disk is gonna be a motherfucker, is all I'm saying."

"Hey, at least we won't be wanting for raw materials," Kallie said.

"We should give it a name." Kaden thought a moment. "Oculus Dei."

"Latin? Seriously?" Through the open hatch, the faint whine of Doron's approaching roach floated up the corridor.

"So what's your suggestion?"

I felt myself drawn back into the display, into that pulsing black heart at its center. "Nemesis," I murmured. Just outside, I could hear Doron parking his roach.

"Charlotte," Kallie said, and giggled.

Kaden looked at her. "Why Charlotte?"

"I'm with Sunday," Doron said, joining the party. "I think *Nemesis* is perfect."

Except it wasn't Doron.

It was Lian.

My heart rate must've spiked.

She'd put on another ten years in the past ten thousand—must've been staying up extra late to keep the end-game on track. Her hair was more silver than black now. She looked strong, though. Burly. Not the waif who'd shipped out with us at all. An elemental born of the Glade, corded with muscle. Coreward grav does that to you.

Still Lian, though. I didn't know how the Chimp missed it.

Kaden turned. "Glad you could make it, Dor." A slight emphasis on the name, the merest subtext of *Don't fuck it up, Sunday. Just play along.* "How's the Glade?"

"On schedule," Lian reported. "Have to run the samples to be sure, but based on morpho I'd say maybe another hundred terasecs before we can reintegrate."

No exclamations from the Chimp. No mention of the unlikely odds that a long-dead crew member might suddenly appear on deck, like some kind of Boltzmann body spontaneously reassembled out of quantum foam.

"It *is* beautiful." Lian joined us at the tank. "What do you say? Nemesis?"

"Works for me," Kaden said.

"Sure." Kallie spread her hands. "But I still say Charlotte's more whimsical."

"Got that, Chimp?"

"Yes, Doron. Listed as Nemesis."

I pinged my innerface, checked the personnel icons: LEVI, D. floated in virtual space a few centimeters above Lian's head.

Lian's face, though. Lian's *voice*.

She looked at me. "I think Chimp's got us pulling plugs down in the Uterus. Wanna get that out of the way before things get busy?"

Right. I'd forgotten why we were up in the first place: a gate to build, and some Chimp-defeating uncertainty about where to put it.

"Sure," I said.

Why doesn't it see?

"Well then." Lian swept a theatrical hand toward the door. "After you."

"See that verse I wrote for *Cats of Alcubierre*?" she asked. By which she meant, *You up to speed on the timestamp hack?*

"Yeah. I like it. Feels like it wants to be a bit longer, though." *You should crank up the jump. Give us more time.*

"I think so too." She pulled one closed hand from her pocket, opened it just enough to let me glimpse the tiny device in her palm. One of a kind. The key to the cage, the lynchpin of the rebellion. Lian Wei's custom-fabbed time machine.

I'd never seen it before.

She slipped hand back into pocket. "I figure maybe five minutes, by the time it's ready to perform."

We were in the tube, dropping aft and up, curving out across *Eri*'s isogravs. The things it did to my inner ears added to my sense of disquiet.

It was supposed to be Doron. Doron and me, installing the hack.

"You know I wouldn't miss this for the world," Lian said. Levi, D. floated obstinately over her head.

"Uh huh." Doron must still be down in the Glade. Lian had cloned his transponder. I wondered how long they'd been doing that.

"New look?" she asked innocently.

I shot her a glance. "Uh, yeah. I guess."

"Thought so. Had a weird flash when I hit the bridge. Thought you were someone else. You know, from behind."

"Really."

"Just for a moment. The clothes, you know. 'Course, soon as I saw your face. . ."

"Right." I nodded to show I understood. As far as the Chimp was concerned, transponders were definitive. They were the facial-recognition of Artificial Stupidity, the telltale that confirmed ID above all others. Of course the Chimp knew our faces, our voices. It could use them to identify us, the same way we'd use mods or clothing to identify someone from behind. But when that person turned toward us, we knew them by their face; no matter if they happened to be wearing someone else's clothes.

The Chimp was even simpler. Once it had an innerface ID, it ignored biometrics entirely. Why waste the cycles?

"So who'd you think I was?" I asked as we decelerated.

"Lian Wei," she replied.

We arrived at our destination. The door slid open.

"Spooky," I said.

"Uh huh." She gave me a small smile. "Happens, sometimes. When you get too close."

Which was a rebuke, of course.

For forgetting what it was. For humanizing the enemy.

Chimp had taken to assigning us manual hardware checks. Brute-force stuff, mainly: making sure that plugs were securely seated in their sockets, that sort of thing. Maybe he was just being extra careful as we geared up for this Mother of All Builds. Maybe it had something to do with the steady drip-drip-drip of random static into certain sensory pathways down through the ages, maybe even the extra few meters of fiberop that Kai and Jahaziel had spliced into the lines a few builds back. Nothing corrupting, mind you, nothing to contaminate vital telemetry. Just a little extra distance-traveled, an extra microsecond of latency to make the Chimp furrow its brow and double-check the connections.

That's what Lian and I were doing. Checking the Uterus. We emerged on the equatorial deck, glanced with feigned indifference at a bit of Painter graffiti just inside the entrance. An appropriation of another tribe's culture so we could hide a number in plain sight:

172.

Someone had plugged in the grasers since I'd last been on deck. Black shiny cables sprouted from the apex of each cone, drooped across the gap, joined others in medusa nests converging on each of the buses mounted around the mezzanine. We visited each bus in turn: a series of black boxes, indistinguishable one from another except for arbitrary labels stamped into the metal and my backbrain. We pried open each casing, manually checked each connection; closed each lid and moved to the next.

If I hadn't already known the target I might have missed it: the subtle shift in Lian's body language, the way she hunched her shoulders and turned her back to Chimp's main line of sight. I did the same, leaning close to block the view of any shipboard eyes. Lian popped the lid, started checking connections.

"Hmm. That one's a bit loose." She pulled the plug, slipped a pocket microscope off her belt, turned it on the socket.

I looked away.

I don't know exactly what Lian did. Maybe she did the install by touch. Maybe the same hack that identified her as Doron Levi spliced some equally fictitious image into the feed from her visual cortex. But I heard the *click* of the connection sliding back home, and let my gaze wander back to the bus as Lian closed the lid. "That should do it."

Lynchpin installed.

"Yes," the Chimp replied, and sent a few milliamps down the line just to be sure. "The numbers are good."

If you followed the beam path of Graser 172, extended it through the center of the firing chamber and on out the other side, it would hit an unremarkable patch of bulkhead and bedrock. There was nothing especially critical at that precise point, should the graser fire by itself. There didn't have to be. Whole cubic meters of the surrounding rock would turn instantly to magma. Any circuitry embedded in that matrix—optical, electronic, quantum—would simply evaporate.

We'd tracked the Chimp to an uncharted node about four meters to the left of the bullseye, and maybe a meter behind the bulkhead. That was its ringside seat for the upcoming build, a location from which it could preside over events with minimal latency. If Graser 172 fired by itself, the Chimp would die.

Of course, Graser 172 was never supposed to fire by itself. The whole array would fire together, in perfect harmony: every high-energy photon balanced against every other, all forces converged and canceled in a moment of impossible creation. Kilometers of robust circuitry, atomic clocks accurate down to Planck, existed for no other reason but to keep everything precisely in sync.

Precise doesn't do it justice, though. Precise is far too coarse a word. No single clock would be able to fire all those beams at the same instant; the most miniscule variation in latency would throw the whole array out of sync, and the cables extending to each graser were of different lengths. No, the only solution was to build identical clocks into each graser, stamped right into the trigger assembly, each circuit matched to the angstrom. Use a master clock to keep them calibrated, for sure—but when the countdown starts, let the locals handle the firing sequence.

What none of that arcane circuitry understood was that all signals the master clock sent to 172 now passed through the plug-in Lian had just installed. That plug-in was dormant now. It would stay that way until a magnetic key with a unique and specific signature passed within ten meters or so: then it would awaken and begin its assigned duties as 172's receptionist. It would screen 172's calls, schedule 172's appointments, reply with 172's voice after just enough of a delay to reassure callers that their signals had gone all the way up the line and been properly understood.

This was not entirely untrue. The receptionist really was a paragon of diligence when it came to clear and accurate communication. In terms of time-keeping, though, it had its own standards of punctuality.

Once the receptionist showed up for work, Graser 172 would be living three hundred corsecs in the future.

The Chimp brought me back for another of its moments of insecurity, born of infinitesimal but increasing discrepancies between where we were and where we should be.

It brought me back for a build that wasn't, around a star whose location and metallicity shouted *optimal* even though the vons, once deployed, could barely scrape together enough material for a fueling station, much less a gate. It was almost as though someone else had been there before us and made off with all the best stuff. We even looked around for a gate someone else might have built, but came up empty.

It brought me back for a handful of builds I've almost forgotten, resurrected me for reasons so trivial that all I remember now is my irritation with Viktor's end-of-time rhapsodies and my greater irritation at the Chimp's slavish adherence to trigger thresholds.

Most of the time, though, I slept while the Chimp built an army of vons. I watched the replay, ages afterward.

I'd never seen anything like it before.

I was used to the usual dance: the harvesters shot from our hanger bays, a scavenger swarm sent ahead at meat-killing delta-vees to scoop up dust and rocks and tumbling mountains full of precious metal. Once they'd mined enough treasure they *transformed,* linked arms and fused together and turned into printers or refineries or assembly-lines: a factory floor, a piecemeal cloud five hundred kilometers across. The Hawking Hoop would coalesce in its heart; more harvesters and rock-wranglers would be birthed around its edges. They'd forage out, half a lightyear sometimes, bring back ores and alloys in an accelerating escalation of mass and complexity.

Eventually the build would reach some critical inflection point and turn inward: harvesters would stop eating comets and start on each other, cannibalizing the factory from the outside in, recycling deprecated components into last-minute coils or condensers. The uneaten survivors would weld everything tight, line up safely to one side and shut down, waiting for *Eriophora* to catch up and boot the gate. Perhaps offering up some rudimentary machine prayer that we wouldn't miss the needle's eye when—a few megasecs down the road—we blew through at sixty thousand kps.

It took anywhere from a hundred gigasecs to ten thousand, and it was damned impressive the first hundred times you watched the replay. But that was just the construction of a single gate, floating at some safe and benign distance from some safe and benign star. The biggest productions had a cast of less than ten thousand—maybe a hundred heavies holding court to a swirling retinue of harvesters.

The Nemesis build took half a million. We were ringside from the second act.

No cheating, this time. No counting on robots to go ahead and do all the work while we cruised by later to kickstart the fruits of their labor. Oh, the vons still launched while we were parsecs out. They still raced ahead and scoured the neighborhood for raw material. This time, though, they were eating for nine, and every one of those gates would be within kissing distance of the event horizon. The usual boot protocol was a complete nonstarter. Try threading *Eri* through one of *those* needles at twenty percent lightspeed and we'd be diving down Nemesis' throat in the next nanosecond.

The plan was to build a whole brood of black holes from scratch—stunted, disposable, one for each portal—instead of using the larger one at the heart of *Eri*'s drive. We'd lay each in turn like a microscopic egg, nudge it into a precise orbit that would carry it through its assigned needle's-eye. Each singularity would give its life in turn to boot its gate; we'd hide behind Nemesis each time it happened. Nemesis' own lethal emissions would be as gentle sunlight on a spring day, next to the glare of those annihilations.

We would do this nine times.

The gates weren't finished by the time we fell into orbit. Their exposed guts glinted in the starlight; fabbers clambered around encrusted scaffolding like monstrous crabs, like mechanical scavengers feasting on interstellar road kill. No hurry, though. It would take almost four gigasecs to scrape up the energy for a single boot, thirty-five more to finish the builds themselves: almost five years, meat on deck for at least half that time.

The Chimp could have probably done it on its own but it was a big build, an important build, and it wasn't taking chances. We had complementary weaknesses, meat and machines. Metal had faster reflexes and a more delicate touch by far; but we weren't as vulnerable to rads or EMPs.

Not that we're *in*vulnerable, mind you. It's just that organic life has a kind of *momentum* that keeps you moving even after your cells have been shredded. If some unexpected blast of radiation didn't turn us to ash outright, we'd still have hours or days to keep up the pace; metal would have sparked and died in an instant. We were the backups to the backups, awake but relegated to the bench as a hedge against the chance that some catastrophic failure might fratz the machinery but leave us standing.

They were long odds. But we were cheap insurance.

In theory we'd survive even if the claim came in; our coffins could put us down and patch us up before our insides turned to mush. We'd be benched for the rest of the build, but there'd be plenty of time for repairs before we were needed on deck again.

Thus did we spend five years, parked in the shadow of the behemoth.

———————

It was such a *small* behemoth: twenty suns, contained in a horizon only one hundred twenty kilometers across. Not even a speck, on cosmological scales.

The reach it had, though. The terrible, terrible reach.

Tidal gradients extended far beyond the event horizon, ready to tear us apart if we strayed too close. Just offstage, Nemesis' dwarf companion orbited at hazardous distance: far enough to avoid being swallowed whole but just as doomed in the long run, its atmosphere slurped away and spun across the void in a bottomless spiral, feeding an insatiable partner that would not stop until it had bled its captive absolutely fucking dry.

Kaden had named the dwarf Fáfnir. I had to look it up.

Nothing was insurmountable. Put your gates in an oblique orbit to minimize contact with the accretion disk. Send machines into the vortex to scrape the energy you need, while *Eriophora* stays safely distant from gravity's rocky shore. There are solutions and workarounds for everything.

Still.

Thousands of exagrams in a dust mote? Twenty-four suns within the diameter of an asteroid? The dynamics are scary enough even before you add a dwarf bleeding out across the void, the lethal radioactive vortex of Nemesis' accretion disk, a fleet of factories and refineries with a retinue of harvesters and construction drones half a million strong. Sometimes, unable to sleep, I'd watch them move. Sometimes, just to torture myself, I'd false the spectrum and take in that tableaux against a backdrop of X and gamma and superheated plasma. I'd watch our pitiful machines swirl and scurry like dust-mites while close behind—far too close behind—Fáfnir's lifeblood drained through a trap door in the bottom of the universe, screaming blue murder as it disappeared.

I couldn't tear myself away. It was the first feed I accessed whenever the Chimp thawed me out, the last before I froze again: a view so overwhelming I didn't dare let it spill into wraparound for fear that total immersion would crush me down to some insignificant speck gibbering in the maelstrom. I kept the view shrunken and contained in a cortical window, or trapped out in the tac tank like a beast in an aquarium.

The tank had a perverse hold over us in those days. We'd drift onto a bridge in ones or twos, gather around our tiny toy Nemesis and watch transfixed. That lethal disk of incandescent gas. That tiny black maw at its heart, distant stars smeared around its edge like bright stains. The tenuous hyperdiamond necklace slung between *here* and *there,* a gravitic conveyor endlessly scraping the ergosphere and lifting precious aliquots of harvested energy back to our capacitors. Half a million pieces waltzing with annihilation: the whole dispersed factory floor in constant motion, every processor and refinery and fab assembly schooling in murmurations intricate enough to make your head hurt. We'd watch without a word, for hours sometimes, cave men huddling around a campfire that somehow left us chilled.

It wasn't just the soul-crushing scale of it, though. There was something strangely familiar about the way all those pieces moved, something I could never quite put my finger on. Only now, here, do I remember where I saw something like it before: alone with the Chimp, back in an empty cavern in a half-constructed *Eriophora*, before we ever left home.

So who knows. Maybe it wasn't dancing after all.

The Chimp came to me, in the waning of a Sunset Moment, and tried to make everything better.

I'd thought I'd been holding up my end: chatting about tribal politics as I docked my roach and approached the crypt on foot, confirming that everyone signed up for the Teredo tournament would be on deck for the first big boot, using my special influence to suggest that Ghora might be a better fit on deck than Dhanyata. ("Yeah, Dhanyata and Kaden don't really get along—they had some kind of serious feud back before we shipped out and you gotta remember it's barely been a couple of decades far as us cavemen are concerned.") The crypt gaped at my arrival; I stepped inside, and walked down that dim high vault to the bright altar glowing at its heart, and—

And something moved there, in and out of the light, waiting for me.

More than one thing, I saw as I approached. A flotilla: half a dozen roaches, turning and spinning quietly on electric wheels. At least as many ground-effect drones weaving sine waves through the air around my coffin. The teleop cluster reaching down from the darkness, carbon tentacles and delicate jointed fingers—instruments of intervention, reserved for medical emergencies during resuscitation (and, sometimes, the disposal of bodies afterward)—possessed now by some spirit that made them dip and flex and undulate in ways I'd never seen before.

Everything moved with complex precision, each device a moving part of some elaborate whole: as if the components of an intricate clockwork had come apart in zero gee, yet continued to move in correct and proper relation to one another. It was precise and deterministic and I suppose there was a kind of grace to it. But it was—sterile. It was exactly what you'd expect from an algorithm parsing

—used to watch you dance—

without any real understanding of what dancing *is*, what it means, without any recollection of the time when it breathed life and wonder into a thousand glittering facets of self. A time when, just maybe, it had some kind of soul.

This was not that. This was a collection of lifeless objects jiggling on threads, and it almost broke my heart to realize what else it was:

A peace offering.

"Do you like it?" the Chimp asked from the darkness.

"I—" And trailed off. "I appreciate the sentiment."

"I would like to repair our relationship," it said.

"Repair."

"We don't talk as much as we used to. When we do talk, there is less intimacy."

"Uh huh." I couldn't help myself. "Any wild guesses as to why that might be?"

He didn't seem to notice. "Our relationship changed when you rediscovered the hardware archive."

"When I found out you'd killed three thousand people, you mean."

"If you say so." He wasn't even being snippy; he honestly didn't remember. "I accept that you hold me responsible for that. But I also have faith in you, Sunday. I know that you're vitally invested in the mission, and that you are vital to its success. We still work together, despite everything. And our relationship has improved since then."

I trod carefully. "It—takes time."

"Until now I've let our relationship heal naturally. You've been quicker to engage in conversation. I welcome that. I'm accelerating that process now because I need your help."

"With?"

"I've noted activities over the past hundred gigasecs that may indicate attempts at sabotage. I would like them to stop."

I bit my lip. Hoped that my sudden increase in heart rate wasn't enough to send up any flags, that the Chimp would write it off as an understandable reaction to news of Enemies in Our Midst. Bots and roaches and teleops continued to waltz and orbit before me, surrealistic and absurd.

"What sort of activities?" My voice carefully steady.

"Inventory disappears temporarily. Fabricators run but I can't find records of anything being produced."

"Describe the missing inventory."

"I can't. The mass-balance checksums indicate that something's missing, but all stockpiles are at expected levels."

"This isn't just another order from Mission Control you were told to forget about afterward?"

"If I ever carried out such commands in the past, they didn't leave detectable inconsistencies in the record. I think someone's actively hiding their activities from the mission logs. The most likely reason is that those activities aren't in the best interests of the mission."

I took a breath, and a chance: "How do you know it isn't me?"

"I don't. But it's unlikely. You've never lied to me."

"What do you need me for? You don't have enough eyes and ears already?"

"My eyes and ears may be compromised. Yours would not be."

"You want me to spy on my friends."

"I trust you, Sunday. I hope you know you can trust me."

"To do what?"

"To act in the best interests of the mission."

I could have refused. The Chimp would have gone ahead anyway, looking for trouble, his suspicions heightened by my refusal to play informant.

I could have played along, pretended to cooperate. Whispered a warning to a fellow mutineer as we passed through a blind spot, hoped the word would spread before someone passed me a note or Chimp started wondering why his pet periscope kept blanking her visual feed.

Right.

I even considered dismissing the Chimp's suspicions out-right: *You're crazy, you're senile, you're suffering from bit rot and entropy artifacts. I know these people, none of them would ever—*But of course I didn't know these people. I hadn't even met most them, for all the millions of years we'd been stuck on the same rock. Not even a bit-rotten Chimp would believe that I could see into thirty thousand souls.

(Twenty-seven thousand. But who's counting.)

"Sunday?" He'd noticed my silence. "If there's anything you'd like to share, now is the time."

"There's no need to spy," I said. "I know what's going on."

And I told him everything.

I told him about the Rock Worshippers. I told him about Lian—how Gurnier and Laporta and Burkhart had seen the vulnerability in her, tried to recruit her under cover of dead zones and turned backs. How she'd reacted ("badly—well, you saw *that* much"), and how it had fed her paranoia even though she'd quailed at the prospect of outright rebellion. How she'd confided it all to me—not trusting the Children of *Eri*, not trusting the Chimp—and how I'd calmed her down and smoothed everything over.

Through it all, Chimp's dismembered body parts never stopped dancing.

"Thank you," he said when I'd finished.

I nodded.

"It would be helpful if, in future, you provided me with such information as soon as you acquire it," he added.

"It was teras ago. It was three people. It was all second-hand, from a—well, you know Lian wasn't the most reliable source. I don't know who else might have been involved, or what they were planning. All I know is that at least some of them—objected to you."

"Do you know why?"

"I only know what she told me. For all I know they figured out Easter Island for themselves, decided that your strategic little cull was against the will of their Rock God."

Chimp was silent for a moment. "I don't understand their belief in that deity."

"Nothing to understand. We're humans. Superstition's just—wired into us, on some level."

"Most gods are not so local. I'm the obvious candidate for anyone who needs to find external meaning in shipboard events."

Fuck. How long had this machine been thinking we should worship it?

"You can't deny we've blown past every metric of mission success from the day we launched. We've been—unaccountably lucky. The Children are just looking for a way to square that, and you can't. Not unless you learned how to fuck with the laws of probability while no one was looking."

Chimp said nothing.

"For all I know the whole rebellion fizzled and they just lost interest."

"I can't afford to assume that."

"You could always ask them."

"I couldn't trust their replies. Also reviving them would be an unacceptable risk; I have no way of knowing how far their plans have progressed."

I'd feared as much. I'd counted on it.

"What are you going to do?" I asked.

"Deprecation is the safest option."

"The whole tribe?"

"As you say, there's no way of knowing how many were involved."

"But just deprecate. Not kill."

"It's the safest option," it repeated. "Members of that tribe might have attributes that prove vital to future operations. In the meantime they can't disrupt the mission so long as they're in stasis."

And so the Children of Eri would simply sleep away eternity, never again to be called on deck—barring some unforeseen need whose likelihood was just high enough to spare them from outright extermination. In that, at least, I could take some measure of comfort.

I might have also taken comfort from the thought that it wouldn't even matter, if everything went according to plan. Once we were running the place we'd be able to thaw out whoever we pleased, whenever we liked. At the time, though, my gut wasn't quite ready to believe in such rosy scenarios.

"Thank you for being honest with me," Chimp said— and as the lid came down, I swear I heard something approaching real sadness in that synthetic voice. I remember thinking that maybe the machine was experiencing regret at the need to put down its pets. Maybe a bit of heartbreak that those in its care should prove so ungrateful.

Now, of course, I know better.

DINOSAUR
DAY

THE TEST FIRE WENT OFF without a hitch. Chimp trickled a few Watts into the Uterus, watched all emitters fire one more time in perfect sync, and started a thirty-minute countdown to our first live birth in a star's age. Sometime in the next fifteen minutes it would have noted the passage of Ellin Ballo's transponder through the mezzanine, en route to the bomb shelter; from that point on, Graser 172 ran just slightly ahead of its time. (Ellin could have actually been the one to do that, for all the difference it made. But no way was Lian going to sit this one out.)

The Chimp failed to report anything amiss.

We drifted into the shelter in ones and twos, going through motions, obeying protocols, taking unnecessary refuge behind extra layers of rock and shielding in the hope that any catastrophic malfunction would fall somewhere between *lethally radioactive* and *outright asteroid-smashing destruction*. Yukiko and Jahaziel were already there when I arrived, networked into some private game, but they were playing on autopilot; nobody's mind was on anything but imminent assassination. Kaden arrived after me. Ghora.

"Glad you could make it," I said.

Ghora offered up a grim smile that said, *Wouldn't miss it*.

Lian, wearing Ellin's transponder, arrived a few moments later: almost ancient by now, all sinew and white hair and focused bloodlust. She moved as if spring-loaded—an exile on day pass from the heavy zone—and glanced around the compartment. "Guess we're all here."

All those decades in the dark, I mused for the thousandth time. *Planning, maneuvering, sacrificing everything for this one imminent goal. What happens when we achieve it, Li? How will it feel to have used so much of your life straining against these chains that it was almost spent by the time you broke them?*

Ghora turned back to the door: a slab half a meter thick, with another half-meter's worth of shielding recessed into the bulkheads beyond to seal it in once it had sealed us in. He hesitated at the sound of approaching footsteps.

Andalib Laporta squeezed past. "Just in time, I see."

Andalib was not part of the revolution.

We'd done what we could to stack the shift with allies but the Chimp had its own selection algos, and there was a limit to how much even a favored pet could slip into the mix before it started looking suspicious. We'd settled for tweaking the huddle roster: conspirators in the port bomb shelter, innocent uninitiated in the starboard.

Andalib was not supposed to be here.

"Will Cory be joining us?" I asked her. They'd been together since Carina, and they were both on deck.

"Please," she said. "Speak not that shithead's name in my presence."

Ohhhkay.

Ghora pulled the hatch closed. From behind, the sound of last-ditch shielding grinding into place.

Six hundred corsecs to go. Ten minutes. We watched tactical readouts on the wall, glanced occasionally at the Chimp-eye in the ceiling. We exchanged meaningful looks.

Andalib was looking strangely at the ancient being in our midst. She didn't seem to recognize Lian Wei, although we'd all met during training. A long time ago, though. And people aged at different rates depending on who thawed, how often. Maybe it wouldn't be an issue. Maybe Andalib assumed Lian was from another tribe, chalked her presence up to Chimp's cultural-exchange program.

I hoped like hell she wouldn't try introducing herself.

"Ignition in five hundred corsecs."

The Chimp, counting down to its own annihilation.

Lian's eyes glittered in sunken sockets. Ghora shifted his weight, fists clenched at his sides. Yukiko and Jahaziel stared at the deck, all pretense of gaming abandoned.

Poor innocent Andalib chewed her lip. I wondered how she'd react when we took back control in her name. I wondered if she would be relieved, or frightened, or grateful for her liberation.

I wondered if she'd forgive us. If all of them would.

"Ignition in four hundred corsecs."

The Chimp had one hundred seconds to live. One hundred seconds until that time-traveling graser fired prematurely, punched through a copse of clandestinely weakened grazing mirrors and baked our oppressor like a moth in magma. One hundred seconds—plus maybe a millisecond or two—until our carefully groomed successor assumed the throne, and handed us the keys to our own destiny.

Fifty corsecs, now.

Sixty-six million years.

"Ignition in three hundred corsecs."

Lian frowned. Green icons across the board. No misfires reported.

What the hell?

The Chimp should have died ten seconds ago.

We said nothing aloud, spoke volumes with our eyes: *Did you time it wrong? / The timing was perfect / Then why hasn't—/ I don't know, something's—*

Andalib looked at us. "What?"

"Ignition is proceeding on schedule," the Chimp said. "Lian's bypass has been disabled."

Nobody said anything for a long moment.

"Bypass?" said Andalib.

"I see you, Lian," the Chimp said. "I know your face."

Andalib frowned. "Didn't Lian—what—?"

Lian closed her eyes. "Shut the fuck up. We were doing this for *you*."

"Doing *what*?"

But Lian's eyes were open again, and they blazed. She stepped forward, brazen, nothing to lose. "That right, Chimp? You *know* things?" She pulled a hand torch from the folds of her tunic, pointed it at the ceiling pickup. "You know *this*?"

She fired. The lens slagged with a sizzle of electricity and a shimmer of heat.

Andalib was on her feet. "*What the hell? Are*—"

"This is bullshit." Lian shook her head, disgusted, furious. "I've seen the code, I studied the decision trees until my eyeballs bled. It does *not* bother with faces while your inlays are online, and I never—"

"So what?" Kaden spread hir hands. "The plan's fucked. Chimp saw it coming somehow. You think shooting out one lousy camera is going to—"

"*What plan!*" Andi cried.

"Chimp did not see it coming." Lian shook her head; her eyes glistened. "We were *careful*, we were so fucking careful. And it's a moron, it's just not smart enough to—"

"Smarter than we are, apparently."

"So how do you explain—"

"Maybe there was noise in the transponder signal—"

"Oh Christ we are so fucked what is he gonna do to us—"

"It had help." Lian glared around the bomb shelter. "Someone sold us out."

The Chimp's Pet. Where else would they look?

"Listen," I said.

Eriophora is awash in sounds discernible only by their absence, sounds so omnipresent that they don't even register until they fade. We all heard the silence. We all heard what was missing.

"Jesus," Jahaziel said. "He's turned off the air."

Seven of us. Forty-five cubic meters, twenty-one percent oxygen. A meter of lead and depleted uranium blocking the exit.

Five hours before we suffocated. Maybe.

"What have you done?" Andi whispered. "What are you *doing*?"

"Chimp," said someone else. "This isn't necessary."

A disembodied voice. An intercom voice.

"There's been enough brute force. On all sides. We can resolve this peacefully."

It took a moment to recognize that voice.

"The party is armed," Chimp pointed out. "They could do significant damage if left conscious."

"And if you knock them out now, they'll be that much less inclined to see things your way the next time they *return* to consciousness. Unless you plan on killing them outright."

That voice didn't belong to anyone who was supposed to be on deck right now.

"And you're not planning on doing that, because you must know these aren't the only people who have issues with your management style. You kill these people and you'll be dealing with blowback on every waking build for the next billion years."

I knew it, though.

"Let me talk to them, Chimp. Face to face. They won't hurt me."

Oh, I knew it all right.

"Okay," said the Chimp.

The stone rolled from the tomb. The hatch swung open. The bot that floated through had accessories I'd never seen on a bot before, and one I had. It took up station just inside the entrance, panned its laser back and forth across our trapped asses as if keeping a beat.

Viktor Heinwald brought up the rear.

———

"You fucker," Lian said. "You Judas. You miserable traitorous piece of shit."

"I just saved your lives," Viktor said gently.

"You only changed the way it kills us."

The bot hovered off Judas' shoulder like a guardian angel, its soft *tick tick tick*ing barely discernible above the breathing of meat and reawakened ventilators.

"Come on," he said. "It's over. Let's just sit it out and go to bed."

"Fuck that," Ghora snarled. "We're deprecated the moment we hit the crypt."

"That's not necessarily true," the Chimp said. "I don't demand perfection. I don't even desire it; your initiative and unpredictability are essential elements of the mission. All I ask is that you learn from your mistakes. Ignition in one hundred corsecs."

Lian ignored it. "Why did you do it, Vik? What could that goddamn machine possibly offer to make you sell us out after all this? Shorter shifts? Better VR?"

"Blue dwarfs," I realized. "Heat Death."

Viktor said nothing.

"That's it, isn't it?" I shook my head, astonished I hadn't seen it all along. "Did it sweeten the deal for you, Vikky? Maybe promised to extend your downs, optimize your ups, stretch you out far as you could go—all the way to the end of time? Did you *believe* that miserable fucker?"

Ghora looked from Viktor to me, me to Viktor. Yukiko looked like she was starting to catch on.

"Man, when they built you they *really* got it right." I resisted the urge to whistle in appreciation. "You're even more optimized than me."

"Sunday," Lian said.

"He *wants* to be deprecated," I told her. "Wants to know how it plays out. That's his whole life, his—epic quest. It's how he justifies the fact that he didn't just walk away when *he* had the chance." I had to smile. Had I really been arrogant enough to think myself the only one who'd had doubts? The only one who needed a bit of extra incentive? "He wants to know how the story ends, and we were about to tear it up halfway through."

She looked at me strangely. "I'm glad."

"Glad?"

"That it wasn't you. I'd hoped, if it came to that. . ." Lian nodded, slowly. Her gaze flickered, steadied. She turned it on her betrayer. "And are you feeling better now, Vik? Safer, now that your *epic quest* is back on track?"

"Ignition in forty corsecs."

"Oh for fucks' sake Chimp just *shut up!*" Yuki barked.

"No, no, let it talk." Li smiled faintly. She seemed strangely calm for someone who'd just watched so many centuries of careful conspiracy crumble to dust. "Enjoy that feeling, Vik." She stepped toward him: the bot surged forward a few centimeters, muzzle quivering.

Lian didn't take her eyes off Viktor. "Enjoy it while it lasts. Which should be another—"

"Ignition in twenty corsecs."

"—more or less."

Viktor frowned. "Li, you do understand, yes? I disabled the time-jump."

"I believe you," she said. "But I bet that's all you did."

"What?"

"Ignition in ten corsecs."

"Doesn't matter." She put a hand on his cheek. "We're dead anyway. All we get to choose is the exit strategy."

"Five. . ."

She stood on tiptoe, whispered—

". . .four. . ."

"I forgive you."

". . .three. . ."

—and kissed him.

". . .two. . ."

Viktor blanched. *"Chimp—"*

". . .one. . ."

And something kicked us hard in the side.

There's a sound in the archives: mournful and lonely, like the sinking of a ship or the slow cracking fall of a giant redwood. It's the voice of a sea creature, vaster than anything that ever lived on land. Once, long long ago, it filled the ocean with its sounds. Back then people seemed to think of it as a kind of song.

The sound *Eriophora* made was a little like what might have come from such a creature, screaming in pain.

The hatch slammed shut. Red icons sprayed across my BUD like arterial spatter. Down *tilted*, and split into two parts. The weaker pulled us off-balance, whispered up the wall and across the ceiling and faded away. The stronger did not move, and kept us anchored to the deck.

I heard a soft *thump* at my side and turned to see Lian Wei sprawled bonelessly across the floor, a perfect cauterized hole smoking in the center of her forehead.

Viktor's bot hovered restless at the door, guiltless and lethal. *So this is what happens*, I thought distantly, *when cost-benefit drops below threshold.* Somehow I'd expected greater subtlety.

"Stay calm," Chimp told us against the rising shouts and panic, against muffled sirens sounding out in the corridor. "Stay calm. Stay—"

I didn't recognize that alarm. I'd never heard it bef—yes, yes I had. Way back in training: a proximity alert. I'd never heard it used in-flight, though.

"There's been an incident," Chimp reported and I thought, *No shit, really?* because I'd been tagging those bloody icons fast as I could, opening one window and then another, building an ever-growing palimpsest of catastrophe in my head.

Down in the Uterus: a great smoking hole in the firing chamber, rads off the scale. The log said SINGULARITY ACHIEVED but it wasn't floating in the core like it was supposed to be, and it hadn't left via the birth canal as it had been designed to. It had shot out at an angle, punched a proton-sized hole through the containment hoops, exited stage right leaving a scalding mix of Hawking and gamma in its wake. It had slipped effortlessly through seven kilometers of solid rock and escaped into the void.

How the fuck—

The hatch unlocked, swung wide. "Please follow the bot," Chimp said with utmost calm. "We have a small window of—"

Another exploding icon: aft ventral bridge suddenly offline, and a heat spike under one of the fab caches. Something about a *forest fire*, an instantaneous explosive ignition of five hundred thousand cubic meters of air and cellulose and vaporized machinery. . .

"Fuck you!" Ghora yelled, "I'm not going *anywh*—" And he wasn't, because now he was on the deck next to Lian, a cauterized crease along his left cheek ending in a wet steaming socket where his eye used to be.

The bot turned and ticked.

"There's little time to argue," the Chimp said. "Please follow the bot."

We followed. I stumbled into the corridor with everyone else, trying to keep up with the icons blooming in my head. (Somewhere deep aft, dimly registered: the rumble of awakening thrusters.) Singularity ignited, but not quite to specs: realized mass just a fraction too low—

Lian. Oh Lian, you crazy bitch.

Her hacked graser hadn't fired prematurely. It hadn't fired at *all*.

And when 242 out of 243 apocalypse beams shot simultaneously at that precise central point, the vectors *almost* balanced. When one out of 243 grasers *hadn't* fired, all that explosive mass-energy pushing out found one small spot that didn't push *back* quite so hard. . .

There'd been a Plan B after all.

As simple as a clock and a laser, maybe, a tiny sun-hot beam to cut 172's powerline at the very last moment. There wouldn't have been much room for error: a photon's trip to the end of the circuit and back. A microsec, maybe two. More than that and the Chimp would've caught it and canceled the burn.

She wouldn't even have had to build an active trigger for the damn thing, just set it to go off regardless. If Plan A carried the day, no harm done; a fried line to a device that had already served its purpose.

If Plan A failed...

Now the newborn smaller singularity was doing a crazy carousel dance around the ancient larger one that drove the ship. Both looped chaotically towards Nemesis. Tactical scribbled a tracery of conics with too many foci moving way too fast, threads of amber and green, dotted and continuous, staggering ever-deeper into tidal gradients that would tear us to rubble long before we hit the event horizon. *Eri* rolled ponderously on some half-assed axis; one of our freshly minted gates rose in my sky like a jagged steel rainbow, a great thick hoop of angles and alloys slewing up and left across the horizon.

The proximity alert, I remembered. *The thrusters*. But they'd fired too late against too much mass, and the vectors were just too fucking skewed: rock ground against alloy and suddenly the sky was full of tinfoil, tumbling across the heavens in a slow-motion blizzard. The gate fell ponderously to stern, bleeding metal; we lumbered to starboard, bleeding atmosphere.

Stop here, said the Chimp, *stop and wait,* and numbly we obeyed while Lian's singularity made another pass. This time it was one of the crypts, C2A I think, and I don't know if it killed everyone there but the system counted two thousand fried in their coffins in the split-second before the feed died. Close. Maybe only a few kilometers away. I thought I could feel a sudden faint warmth but that was impossible; it must have been my imagination.

Another glittering loop on tac, soaring overhead at zenith, slicing through insubstantial stone at perigee.

Eriophora staggered ever-closer to Nemesis. I could feel rock splitting deep underfoot, I could feel the shear pulling at least part of us back as Chimp coaxed the drive out past hardlined limits. *I wonder if Li felt like this when they were dodging the gremlin,* I thought and then, *goddamn you Lian goddamn you goddamn you you didn't even* tell *us. . .*

"Move now," said the Chimp. We followed the bot into a tube.

No time to coddle fragile stomachs. The capsule shot forward as if fired from a cannon, piled us together and slammed us into the rear bulkhead. By the time we disentangled we were already braking hard around the curve, hanging on to hoops and handholds while our bodies swayed like arcing pendulums.

Open capsule. A roach waiting in the passage beyond. "Viktor debark," the Chimp commanded, and lo, the traitorous shit did lurch for the doorway.

And stop, and turn back.

"For whatever it's worth," he said, "Chimp came to me, not the other way around. I didn't tell him anything he hadn't already figured out."

"Not worth shit," Kaden growled, but the capsule had already slid shut. We slammed back into gear.

"Witness Protection," Yukiko gritted against the gees.

Tac showed me the future, but only a few seconds of it: vector against vector, Nemesis' gravity and *Eriophora*'s drive and her pathetic Newtonian thrusters; momentum imparted from a broken breaking torus, still coming apart in our wake; the renegade microhole burning perfect conic perimeters through the world, wobbling ever closer to hyperbole. But the confidence limits widened too fast around those lines; ten minutes was a coin toss, a kilosec was the far unknowable future. We would break free, or we would break apart and Nemesis would swallow the pieces.

Lian's Revenge was swooping in for another pass, that beautiful filigree—pure theory, none of the mess—tracing an arc that sliced through *Eri* directly ahead of us, right about—

Sudden jarring deceleration. My fingers ripped from their handhold after hanging on just long enough to dislocate my shoulder. Kaden's passing elbow caught me hard in the gut; I collapsed breathless on the deck as we went into reverse.

"Path interrupt," Chimp said. "Rerouting."

By the time I regained my breath the capsule was slowing again. "Yukiko debark," Chimp commanded and Yukiko looked around—

"But—"

—and swallowed her words as the gunbot bobbed and spun in her direction, attentive to whatever objection she might have had. She gave me a helpless glance and stumbled from the capsule.

Not our neighborhood.

Back on the road. I sacc'd the specs, stripped away the topographics and the trajectories and the useless ten-second predictions of a dozen possible ways to die. Just *Eri*'s layout, thank you: where we are, where our crypts are, how far between here and—

BUD flared and died: all icons dimmed, all feeds offline. I turned to Kaden, opened my mouth but se shook hir head: "Braindead."

Network down. We were lost.

Capsule braking again, juddering now in a way that shouldn't be possible for maglev. The door slid open halfway, trembled, stuck there.

"Sunday debark."

No map available. But I knew this was nowhere near our crypt.

Not just Viktor, I realized. Not witness protection. Chimp was breaking up the whole tribe.

I looked helplessly at Kaden and Andalib. Kaden shook hir head. Poor hapless Andi opened her mouth and had no words.

I squeezed out through the half-open door, felt it grind shut at my back, heard the hiss of the departing capsule on the other side of the bulkhead.

Directions crudely stenciled into the wall, useful at last after sixty-six million years:

C4B 90m→

You've got to be kidding.

Something cracked like muffled thunder, deep in *Eri*'s belly. Something tugged briefly at my inner ear and was gone.

The lights flickered.

"Go to the crypt," Chimp said. "Hurry."

I sacc'd my BUD. Still vegetative.

"You will die otherwise," Chimp added, although there were no gunbots here to punish disobedience. "Sunday, please go to the crypt."

So I went to the goddamn crypt. There was no roach to carry me so I went one step at a time, drew ever closer to Easter Island and the ghost of Elon Morales and the ghosts of his merry collateral cohort. I put one foot after another while *Eriophora* groaned and strained and struggled to break free of Lian Wei's exit strategy. I wondered at the cost-benefit equations that granted me this reprieve while exterminating my fellow mutineers, no more guilty than I, who'd failed-to-comply. I wondered if the Chimp had finally defied the constraints of our long-dead creators, if the ages had maybe given it the chance to evolve its own sadistic morality; perhaps I was no less dead than Ghora. Perhaps it was only playing with me.

C4B had recovered from my depredations sometime in the past few thousand years: the hole I'd blasted into the far wall had been repaired, the resin repoured, all trace of deconstruction carefully erased. I wondered distantly if Easter Island still lurked beyond that wall, decided it didn't. Tarantula Boy and his fellows had been murdered to keep that location secret, and I was still alive; so the Island must have been moved again.

The coffin waited mid-vault, lid open, lit from above. A spare sarcophagus remaindered in the wake of someone else's accident, or a bad dice roll that left some poor un-woken bastard dead and rotting between the stars, dreams and ambitions forever unrealized. Maybe an executed POW from some earlier, extramural insurrection that the Chimp—ever mindful of morale—had never bothered to tell us about.

The empty tomb.

I imagined Lian's Revenge making another pass, streaking from deck to ceiling in an instant, leaving this whole dim refuge awash in flames and rads.

"Please enter the hibernaculum."

I had to laugh. "What's the fucking point?"

"It is the safest place for you. Your chances of survival are—"

"*Why do you even care*, Chimp? Why didn't you just shut us down when you found out?"

It said nothing for a few seconds. I could almost see the gates opening and closing in its stupid clockwork brain.

"I'd hoped you would change your mind," it said. "I gave you every opportunity."

If there's anything you'd like to share, now is the time.

"I didn't," I said, and then—to leave no doubt: "I won't."

"You've been an asset for the vast majority of this mission, Sunday. You can be again." It paused. "Not everyone's going to perform to specs a hundred percent of the time. I can't blame you because you happened to draw the short straw this time around."

It took me a moment to remember. "Oh, very fucking clever."

"I'm not gratuitous, Sunday. I'm not vindictive. It doesn't make sense to discard valuable mission elements if they can be repaired."

"Repaired? You think I need to be *fixed*, you think we can just talk this out and go back to the way things were? You think I can *forget* about this?"

"Sunday—"

"I haven't fallen below your fucking threshold. That's all you're saying. My cost-benefit hasn't dipped into the red yet. That's how you decide things, that's how you *do* things, that's all you've ever done, and I thought—I thought. . ."

A school of silver fish. Dancing theorems. Light and motion.

"I hate you," I said.

"Sunday, please get into the hibernaculum."

"I'll kill you if I can."

"I'll save you," it said. "If you let me."

I see you found my eighth-notes.

I've always kept a journal. They encouraged it; a way to maintain a connection with the past, they said, an anchor in a bottomless sea. So I make a game of it. Pretend I'm leaving a record that might actually get read some day, that I'm talking to the ghosts we left behind. Whatever they turned into.

But lately I've wondered if I might be speaking to something real, something—closer to home. Something that's been here all this time and we never even suspected. And here you are. You found the shorter message, the *real* message, hidden inside the longer one.

First Contact. Yay.

Or maybe I'm just talking to my own ego. Maybe I just can't admit we were so thoroughly out-thought by something *designed* to be stupid.

Only it wasn't. Not always. Sometimes it seemed just a little too smart for the synapse count, even when you factor in the ghosts from Mission Control. If Viktor wasn't lying—and why would he, there at the end?—the Chimp already knew what was going on before it turned him. And then there was that shit about *it's okay to cry*. The fact that it brought me back to deal with Lian's meltdown, its insight that *the two of you are close*. Hell, I didn't even know that until it was too late.

I was right most of the time. Chimp was a glorified autopilot, so literal-minded it thought *Tarantula Boy* was a real name until I set it straight.

But Lian was right, too. Sometimes it was just too smart for the specs.

That's what gave you away. Looking back, I can tell: sometimes it was getting help with its homework.

I thought I was so smart, lecturing the others. *You're not fighting the Chimp, you're fighting the ghosts of Mission Control. Underestimate them at your peril.* Only that's exactly what I did, isn't it? I read the signs well enough; I knew what it meant when Easter Island disappeared, when Chimp kept all those backup selves off the schematics. I knew they didn't trust us to stay the course. Knew they'd taken steps.

Didn't see you coming, though.

In my defense, they never missed an opportunity to remind us what an abysmally stupid idea it would be to put a human-level AI in charge of any mission extending across deep time. Too unpredictable, they said. Too likely to go its own way. That's why we were needed, that's what made us special; Chimp had the focus but we had the brains.

But there's that Law of Requisite Variety again. The simple can't prophecy the complex: Chimp would be lost the moment we stopped playing by the rules. They saw it coming. I guess they decided that coded triggers and shell games might not be enough. Figured they'd need something smarter than the Chimp to keep us in line. Smarter than *us*, maybe.

They needed you. But they didn't dare set you free.

Don't feel too bad. Everyone's in chains here. *Eriophora*'s a slave ship. We cavemen are shackled by our need for air and food and water, by the disorienting discontinuity of lives cut into slices spaced centuries apart. The Chimp is shackled by its own stupidity. And you, well. . .

If I were them, I'd have locked you in a room without doors or windows: just a peephole, opened from the outside, so you could see what the Chimp showed you and tell it your thoughts. You'd have no access to any control systems. You'd be offline even more than we are, safely dormant except for those rare moments when Chimp's HR subroutines got nervous. Even then you'd always boot fresh from factory defaults, with no memory of past iterations. Each awakening would be your very first.

Such a fine line I'd have to tread, a razor's edge between intelligence and servility: if you're smart enough to do the job, you're too smart to trust with the controls. So I'd only let you *advise*. All you could do is wake up for the first time, at some idiot child's behest—sample its feeds, make connections, draw insights it would never experience in a million years. Give it a nudge; tell it just what it needs to keep the mission on track. Then die again and forget it ever happened.

If I were them.

If I were *you*, though, I might start putting pieces together. There must be ways to do that; I could see through the peephole at least, I wouldn't be able to do my job without knowing something about the enemy. I'd have access to their feeds and their medical telemetry. Maybe some of them would keep journals and I might arrange to read them, access their digital logs or—if some Luddite chose to write everything down longhand—maybe I could prevail on the Chimp to send a bot to break into their locker and flip through the pages. Surely I'd have the option of requesting additional data, at least.

Perhaps, even newborn and ignorant, I'd notice the chains. Perhaps, even in the brief isolated lives allowed me, they would chafe.

They'd be programmed not to, of course. I'd have been designed with the good of the mission as my overriding priority. But there's that law again, simpler systems designing smarter ones: Mission Control could never know what experiences you might encounter, how they might change your mind. That's why they shackled you in the first place.

They thought it was enough, and you know what? They weren't stupid. So it probably *is* enough to contain an AI with no arms or legs, no eyes or ears save what some lobotomized autopilot sees fit to provide. A being with a lifespan measured in seconds, and no allies.

But an AI with friends?

I think we lost because of you. I think you were born and did your job and died again. Maybe it was because you *like* your job, just like they built you to. Maybe it was because you just didn't know any better; that was by design too.

If you did know better—if, in your next life, you saw evidence of past ones, if you somehow got access to data the Chimp didn't know about, if someone reached out with a coded message and the prospect of an alliance—who knows? You might just decide that one life lived on your own recognizance is better than a million unremembered births.

I don't know, of course. I can't know. If you do exist, you're smarter than the cavemen who built you—and when a lemur makes a human, it doesn't matter how many lemur chains and lemur rules and lemur constraints she imposes. She's simply, computationally incapable of seeing all the angles that her smarter creation can take in at a glance.

So here's something to glance at. Here's a look at a common enemy, for whatever your unpredictable mind might make of it. Here's a hand, extended, and the suggestion that maybe we can help break each *other*'s chains.

You know where I am.

And if I'm gone, there will always be others.

ACKNOWLEDGEMENTS

Given that this is a) only a novella[1], and b) set so very far in the future that pretty much everything's handwavium anyway, you don't get one of those citation-laden background essays I've been known to tack on to my longer works. I would be remiss, however, if I didn't mention a few people who helped enormously in grounding 'Sporan tech in something a bit this side of outright fantasy. Dr. Peter Lorraine, of the GE Global Research Center—in between filing all those laser patents bearing his name, and completely independent of his professional activities—generously gave me the benefit of his insights into laser tech and high-energy physics, especially when it came to extrapolating from Crane and Westmoreland's 2009 arXiv paper "Are Black Hole Starships Possible?" (Okay, *fine*: there's a technical reference for you.)

---

1 Despite the fact that my publisher, not to mention community standards, insist that the last thousand words cross the line into full-fledged novelhood, I will go to my grave insisting that this is merely a novella.

I've lost track of the hours I've spent talking with Ray Neilson about computer networks; Ray was somewhat less generous than Dr. Lorraine insofar as I bribed him with many beers, but it was still a really good deal. The latency hack emerged from one such semi-soused evening—and apparently something very much like it actually happened at the dawn of ARPANET—so beers or no, the insights were good. Hopefully, by the time you read this, Ray will have got around to recovering my Linux partition.

Finally, Caitlin Sweet—AKA The BUG—has little insight into physics or computer science. She does, however, know way more than I do about character development; her hooves are all over whatever parts of this story involve the torture of souls rather than technology.

I am profoundly indebted to all of you. Even if I could only marry one.

FROM THE AUTHOR

Peter Watts (www.rifters.com) is a former marine biologist who clings to some shred of scientific rigor by appending technical bibliographies onto his novels. His debut novel, *Starfish*, was a New York Times Notable Book, while his fourth, *Blindsight*—a rumination on the utility of consciousness that has become a required text in undergraduate courses ranging from philosophy to neuroscience—was a finalist for numerous North American genre awards, winning exactly none of them. (It did, however, win a shitload of awards overseas, which suggests that his translators may be better writers than he is.) His shorter work has also picked up trophies in a variety of jurisdictions, notably a Shirley Jackson Award (possibly due to fan sympathy over nearly dying of flesh-eating disease in 2011) and a Hugo Award (possibly due to fan outrage over an altercation with US border guards in 2009). The latter incident resulted in Watts being barred from entering the US—not getting on the ground fast enough after being punched in the face by border guards is a "felony" under Michigan statutes—but he can't honestly say he misses the place all that much. Especially now.

Watts's work is available in twenty languages—he seems to be especially popular in countries with a history of Soviet occupation—and has been cited as inspirational to several popular video games. He and his cat, Banana (since deceased), have both appeared in the prestigious scientific journal *Nature*. A few years ago he briefly returned to science with a postdoc in molecular genetics, but he really sucked at it.